THE COWARD

GARY KHAN
A KRYPTIC NOVEL

authorHOUSE

AuthorHouse™ UK
1663 Liberty Drive
Bloomington, IN 47403 USA
www.authorhouse.co.uk
Phone: 0800 047 8203 (Domestic TFN)
+44 1908 723714 (International)

© *2020 Gary Khan. All rights reserved.*

No part of this book may be reproduced, stored in a retrieval system, or transmitted by any means without the written permission of the author.

Published by AuthorHouse 12/11/2019

ISBN: 978-1-5246-3449-0 (sc)
ISBN: 978-1-5246-3450-6 (hc)
ISBN: 978-1-5462-9370-5 (e)

Print information available on the last page.

Any people depicted in stock imagery provided by Getty Images are models, and such images are being used for illustrative purposes only.
Certain stock imagery © Getty Images.

This book is printed on acid-free paper.

Because of the dynamic nature of the Internet, any web addresses or links contained in this book may have changed since publication and may no longer be valid. The views expressed in this work are solely those of the author and do not necessarily reflect the views of the publisher, and the publisher hereby disclaims any responsibility for them.

Contents

Chapter 1	The Cotton Field	1
Chapter 2	The Letter	13
Chapter 3	The Fetching Ceremony	22
Chapter 4	The Coward	32
Chapter 5	The Two Roads	47
Chapter 6	The Ol' Weston	65
Chapter 7	The Sage	77
Chapter 8	The Call	83
Chapter 9	The Lady of the Canyon	89
Chapter 10	The Concept of Hell	100
Chapter 11	The Mountain	108
Chapter 12	The Wolves	119
Chapter 13	The Bregfurjen	124
Chapter 14	The Coward	133

This book is dedicated to Nix,
the driving force behind this Story,
and to Katy Kate, its fierce editor.
Where would this story be without you?

1

The Cotton Field

Talon jerked awake screaming. His abdomen seared, and his insides erupted spewing volumes of black-blood in all directions. He fumbled in the dark, panicked. He was going to die. The endless stars in the sky shrank away into a blur and then snapped back into crisp focus with every breath he took. He coughed, choking on the hot coals caught in his throat, momentarily silencing his screams. His hand clasped on to something.

'Don't move,' someone said.

His entire body convulsed. His face twisted, and his eyes bulged. He used every inch of strength in him to lift his head off the hard floor. A shadowy figure lurked over his middle covered in his blood. Too much blood. He was definitely going to die.

'You hold on now boy,'

The earth shook beneath him and let out a harrowing, icy wail that sent horrible shivers through his very being. It was coming from his lips and continued for what felt like a lifetime, an eternity of agony. His throat recoiled as his voice broke cutting, muzzling his desperate pleas for life, for reprieve.

The shadow dug its hands into Talon's abdomen forcing his back to arch violently and sending cascading waves of pain quivering through his entire body. Thick veins formed at the edge of his temples as his eyes rolled back into his head.

It was day and then night and then blackness and then light, he couldn't tell. Then there was only darkness and pain.

'I know it hurts,' the deep voice said from far away in the abyss. 'but you have to stop moving or I might kill you.'

Talon opened his mouth to speak. Instead, he let out a heart-rending howl. His heart thrashed wildly against the inside of his chest like a mad beast trying to flee its cage.

'SSSTOPP!' Talon gasped between clenched teeth.

'Just a little longer boy,'

Talon tried to protest but there were no words, no meaning, no existence. Only agony. Only endless torment - the torrential coursing of bone-biting, breaking, magma burning through his veins. Sweat dripped off him in buckets. His skin bubbled and boiled, as though he were trapped in a furnace, where the flames greedily licked at his skin.

'H-h-hellpp m...' Talon cried.

'King be damned!' the figure hissed. He ripped his sleeve free from Talon's grasp.

'You have a women boy?'

Talon cried loudly.

The shadow removed his hand from Talon's gut. Talon screamed.

'THINK OF HER NOW!'

Talon whimpered and gargled. His head split in two preventing him from focusing. There was only pain. How could he think?

The figure placed a bloody palm on Talon's forehead.

'Think of her...'

Talon opened his eyes. He stood on a shallow embankment on the edge of a wild cotton field. Tall stalks of grass ran in all directions scattered with the reds, purples, and yellows of wild and exotic flowers. A strangely sweet scent hung in the air, emanating from the natural bouquet.

In between the flowers, tall stalks rose about shoulder-height. Large balls of cotton clung lazily to the edge of these stalks. A soft breeze caressed the back of his neck as it passed over the field. It didn't take much to liberate the balls of cotton from their stalks. The effect reminded Talon of the first snowfall at the end of autumn.

At the bottom of the embankment, the shallow Hexon River snaked towards Hexon Falls, the water feature his village was named after, and the place where most of the village children swam during summer. The river gurgled along and the waters splashed against the odd rock. Crickets sang from behind the curtain of tall grass, while the red robins chirped away in willow trees that ran along the river's edge. A stray bee buzzed past his head.

'Hiya Tal,'

He swung around.

'Kat!'

Before he could react, she leaped into his arms and the moment had them spin around before falling into the tall turf.

'I missed you today,' she said lying next to him in their bed of grass. 'Choirs, apprenticeships, errands were just plain boring as usual. That's village life I guess.'

'My day was horrible as usual,' he said.

'The bullies again?'

He nodded.

'I don't know why you don't stand up for yourself Tal,' Katrina said. She rolled on to her side and frowned at him. Her eyes, a piercing tea-green, scolded him.

'I know,' he said. 'I will.'

She laughed a sigh of a laugh and fell back on to her pillow of light golden-blonde curls. She grabbed his hand in her own and interlocked their fingers. Her laugh was contagious. Talon found himself chuckling along with her. Her laugh was his favourite sound.

She turned her head towards him and he turned his head towards hers. Both smiling. The sun danced off her tanned skin. It always fascinated him how her skin could glow the way it did. He took her in, all of her. She was the most beau….

'KAATTT!' he screamed.

'BE STILL,' the deep voice said.

His abdomen burned, but a blanket prevented him from seeing what was happening. It seemed lighter, but he still couldn't tell if it was day or night.

He twisted his body, and his muscles knotted and spasmed as he recoiled from the pain. He kicked dust into the air and dug his nails into the dirt to brace against the excruciating sensation ebbing from his centre.

How was he still alive? He shouldn't be alive. Not with this pain.

'MAKE IT…' he began.

'Easy now,' the voice interjected. 'Focus on the place you were just now. Focus on your loved ones. I promise you don't want to be awake for this next part.'

'Wha -,' Talon hoisted his head to catch a glimpse of what he meant.

He hit his head roughly on the ground as he whipped backwards roaring until his voice broke again, and still he let out a silent scream, clenching his body together.

The wet palm touched his forehead again and then there was nothing...

'Get him!' someone shouted.

Talon's foot sank into a muddy puddle. The dirty water splashed across his worn corduroy trousers. Stumbling, he crashed into Mr Balich's orange stand, cartwheeled over the counter and sent oranges spraying in all directions.

'TELMACHE YOU FOOL!' the old man howled after him, but Talon disappeared around the corner.

He found himself on Teller's Bend, one of the main streets in his village, Hexon Falls.

'Over there boys!' a voice shouted from behind him.

Talon didn't look back. He cut left into the adjacent cobbled street and was forced to weave between a single-horse carriage and a group of women. The women gasped as he forced his way through.

'Watch it you scoundrel!' someone shouted after him.

Talon glanced back for the first time, but the crowded street obscured his vision. At the top of the road, he paused and took his bearings. He was on Baker's corner. The smell of Mr Borden's famous mince pastries filled the streets. Talon took a moment to catch his breath and filled his nostrils with air and with it came the intoxicating scent of honey and fresh bread.

A familiar whistling announced his pursuers. He turned to run, but crashed into a peeved shopper, who fell to the ground as he did.

'Sorry, so sorry,' He said bouncing to his feet.

He sprinted down Stable Lane towards the low wooden building three or four houses wide where the village tanner, Miss Penny made shop.

'Hiya, Talon!' Miss Penny said waving, as he dashed past.

He waved quickly and turned the corner. He raced down the squint road, which slanted upward slightly because of the enormous knobbed roots of the giant fir tree. Talon didn't see anyone behind him or hear the bullies. He slowed down cautiously. He was hit by the smell of wet wood and old dirt. His shoes clicked loudly on the cobblestone. The street was suspiciously quiet. He turned down the last alley that lead home but was cut off before he reached the end.

'Gotcha!' a burly boy huffed.

'Dane,' Talon said. He turned to bolt back the way he came but once again was cut off by Dane's accomplices, Jones Mayton and Reed Horne.

'Guys, come on,' Talon said.

'Little birdy told us you callin' me a fat... toad... Telmache,' Dane said. He spat heavily. 'That true?'

'No,' Talon said.

'Liar,' Dane replied. Dane, a tall boy made of more fat than muscles, stood a head taller than Talon and was at least twice as wide. His belly hung out over his pants and his shirt buttons strained to contain his girth. The large bully stalked closer as Talon edged backwards. 'That's what you is, huh Telmache, a sorry goat sack of a liar.'

'No, I'm not,'

'Oh so you admit, you been callin' me names?' Dane said. 'Knew I could get the truth out of you.'

'I don't want to fight you,' Talon said.

The boys roared with laughter.

'You never fight you coward,' Jones said. He pushed Talon forward towards Dane.

'Yeah you sissy,' Reed said.

'I'm not a sissy,' Talon shouted.

'Prove it,' Dane said. 'Fight.'

'No,'

'Maybe that's why your girlfriend been cosying up to the prince, ey? You too much of a sissy for her,' Dane said. He cracked his knuckles, tilted his head and licked his lips greedily.

'What?' Talon said.

Reed pushed Talon forward again. They closed in around him.

'The prince and Kat,' Jones said.

'What about them?' Talon asked.

The boys roared with laughter again.

'Oh, he don't know!' Reed said.

'Tell me,' Talon hissed.

The bullies chuckled.

'Why don't you find out – ' Reed began.

'Hey!' Dane interrupted. 'I do the talking.'

Reed swallowed audibly. 'Sorry.'

'Seems pretty little Kitty Kat go be princess Kitty Kat,' Dane said. He smirked at the look of confusion on Talon's face. 'You goat sack of a fool – Kitty Kat is goin' marry them prince Calren.'

'Probably be Queen Kitty Kat one 'em days too,' Jones said.

'Liars!' Talon said. 'She wouldn't.'

'What?' Dane asked. 'You thought she'd marry a miserable worm like you?' You're BIG...FAT... UGLY... LIARS!'

Dane's face turned crimson and his cheeks swelled to almost double their normal size.

'Wha'did you say, you...' Dane filled his chest with air and swaddled forward.

Jones and Reed cackled.

'NO...ONE...CALLS...ME....FAT!'

Jones and Reed each grabbed one of Talon's arms and held him in place. Dane wound his arm back and clenched his fat hand in to a fist...

'One last step boy,' the voice said to him, but it was as if it were on the other side of eternity. He couldn't see anything. There was just emptiness. Endless emptiness. Somewhere in the emptiness pain, anger and hurt echoed.

'Just breathe,' the voice said.

He heard screams – thousands upon thousands unrelenting, tortured screams, crashing against the black cliffs of life and death.

... Darkness

The endless void pressed in from all sides making it harder to breathe...

Talon tried to thrash around, but his body wouldn't move. Far off on distance shores...

The dark agony swam ceaselessly in the emptiness threatening to drown him.

He heard the faint and remote sighs of Kat's voice from behind the black veils serenading him. He felt her breath on the back of his neck.

Again, he heard his name. A whisper in the ever-dark. A voice or the wind? It called to him...

Darkness...

...Pain.

Nothing...

Burning. Talon felt a jolt and then unrelenting burning. A deep sense of it spread across his body. A raging inferno, centred deep within him somewhere much closer in the darkness which shifted giving way to a hot summer's day...

Talon was on the far side of the Cotton Field back home, watching from a distance two figures laying in the grass, holding hands and laughing. The girl had long blond curls, the boy a tangled mess of brown hair. They were looking at each other. Why didn't they notice the heat? Unnatural waves of warmth swelled over the scene. The lazy cotton floating in the sky caught ablaze and burnt through quickly leaving only swarms of dead ash dancing unceremoniously around the hot skies.

Burning. The ash touched the green blades of grass and ignited it, sprouting flames wherever it fell. The field itself became a raging inferno, the flames reaching desperately for the sky. Everything was on fire. He had to warn the two people in the field. They would be caught in the blaze. Why didn't they notice it? It was so hot.

Burning. The fire reached them and swept across them like a torrent. His own skin pealed in the unbearable heat, the flames, melting him, flesh and bone. Why didn't they notice it? It stung, every fibre of him rang out in alarm. Someone was screaming. A familiar voice resonated through the heat, thick in the air.

Talon shrieked, and growled, and cried, slamming his fist into the ground in violent submission to the pain. He cried a last and final cry, cried for hell and for heaven and for the end of all things.

'Oh Talon, where have you been you silly boy,' His grandmother said as he entered their home. 'Not again.'

He held his side which ached. Streaks of dried blood wiped away by a muddy sleeve told his grandmother everything she needed to know, as did the dark ring around his eye.

'I will have a strong word with that fat ingrate's parents,' his grandmother said. 'Sit.'

She pointed to a chair at the kitchen table and disappeared into her pantry. The smell of her boiling potato stew made his stomach grumble. He heard the distinct clanking of vials and bottles where his grandmother rummaged for something. He sank into the rickety old chair and took a few deep breaths. The pot bubbled happily on the large furnace. The buzzing of people could be heard outside the kitchen window which looked out onto the street, but the grime on the outside prevented him from looking out.

'Here we go,' his grandmother said, sinking into the seat closest to him. She placed several vials on the kitchen table top. 'Drink these in this order.'

He complied, while she soaked a cloth in a potent oil that stung his nostrils, and equally stung his skin when the elderly woman placed it on the place he had been hit. It burned for a moment or two and then all the pain evaporated.

'What was it this time?'

'Someone told Dane, I said he looks like a fat toad,'

'There is a lot of truth to that statement,' His grandmother winked at him. 'But never mind that now. I have a surprise.'

He looked at her expectantly.

'Kittie is back,' she smiled.

He made to jump up, but she forced him back into his seat.

'You are not leaving this house looking like that,' she said. 'We've been invited for dinner by the Darringers, and you will look presentable, now go wash up.'

Talon smiled. Kat was back.

He and his grandmother stood outside the largest house in the village an hour later. He held a pot filled with his grandmother's delicious stew waiting excitedly. Someone shouted from inside. There was a loud noise and the large brown door opened and there stood Katrina Darringer, as beautiful as ever wearing a long summer dress.

'Talon!' she shouted excitedly. She grabbed him in a bear hug almost forcing the pot in his hands to fall.

He moaned in pain but chuckled, 'Hello Kat.'

She stepped back. 'What's wrong? Bullies again Tal?'

He nodded.

'And I am here too Kittie,' his grandmother said with a raised eye.

'Oh, so sorry Blithe, hello.' She hugged the older woman and welcomed them in. 'We are about to sit down at the table.'

The house was as well decorated as Talon remembered, far more lavish than their old home. They headed straight to the dining room, where a full spread of food had been laid out.

'You sit here, next to me Talon,' Kat said.

Everyone else joined them in the dining room. Mrs Darringer, Kat's mother, entered first. A tall woman, still holding on to her youthful beauty with the same golden curls as her daughter. Mr Darringer entered after her, a large grizzly man, with a thick black beard.

'Talon,' he said briskly.

'Hello Mr Darringer,' Talon said. The man sniffed.

'Hello Tal,' Mrs Darringer said, giving him a light hug. 'Good to see you again.'

'Hi Mrs Darringer, thank you, same,' he replied.

'Blithe darling, come sit next to me,' Mrs Darringer said.

Kat took the pot from Talon and put it on the table. 'There is someone I want you to meet Tal,' she began saying.

'Ah, Calren my boy,' Mr Darringer said loudly. 'Come, come, you will sit next to me!'

A handsome, well-built young man with blonde-brown hair stepped into the room. He was well dressed in the finest clothes Talon had ever seen and he wore a robe in the same mauve of the royal family.

'Everyone, may I introduce prince Calren, the future king of our land,' Mr Darringer said with his chest swollen. He glanced at Talon with a smirk on his face.

The prince made his rounds and greeted everyone.

'Talon, right?' he said shaking Talon's hand. 'Kat has told me so much about you, in fact she never stops talking about you and the adventures the two of you shared.'

Talon remained silent. The entire room did.

'Boy, you better bow before I come over there,' his grandmother said.

'Ah, no need for formalities, please,' Prince Calren said. 'Really.'

'Nice to meet you,' Talon whispered. He looked at Kat. She beamed at the two of them shaking hands. For a moment it felt like the earth had given way under him, and then Mrs Darringer invited everyone to take their seats. Talon sunk into his chair, slightly dazed.

The flames from the candles danced in response to the movement. The yellow light emanating from the table created abstract shadows on the walls, but it illuminated all the smiling faces at the table, all smiling except for Talon. Dane's words echoed throughout his mind the entire time.

'Let's eat,' Mr Darringer chuckled.

Kat was caught in a conversation with Blithe who sat on the other side of her. Talon caught hints of the conversation. Something about her studies at the capital, and how well they were going, and something about a ball. They ate, but he didn't lift a single thing off his plate.

'So, Tal, how are you?' Kat asked. 'I'm sorry we haven't had a chance to chat properly yet. Everyone is so excited about me being back.'

Talon looked at her. His expression was confused.

'You haven't eaten anything,' She said. 'Are you okay?'

He didn't answer.

'Tal?'

'What is he doing here?' he whispered to her. He nodded at Prince Calren. The table went silent.

'Well that is what this dinner is for,' Kat stuttered. 'Prince Calren and I have an announcement to make and we wanted to tell the people we loved the most first.'

'What announcement,' Talon felt sick in his stomach.

Kat stood up and went around the table to Prince Calren. He stood up and they locked hands. Mrs Darringer, gasped and put her hands over her mouth. Mr Darringer beamed as though he could not be prouder if he dared. His grandmother, looked at him with a concerned expression on her face.

'Calren and I would like to formally announce to you all, our family and friends that we are going to get married,'

There was an electrifying buzz in the room. Everyone jumped up at the same time and went to congratulate the couple.

'My darling, my darling!' Mrs Darringer repeated.

'Well done my boy,' Mr Darriner said to Prince Calren.

Talon got up slowly, turned around and headed for the door and slipped out of the house. He walked through the streets where the sound of laughter and lazy merriment washed over him. He struggled to breathe and walked without sense of direction.

'Talon!' Kat shouted after him.

Without looking he ran, as fast as he could. The dinner played through his mind like a bad dream, his worst dream. He ran faster still until he hit the treeline of the forest. Talon stampeded through the trees cursing loudly. His shirt sleeve caught on a branch. He tore it free. Another branch caught him in the face. A stray thorn cut his cheek. Windswept and out of breath, Talon broke free of the last bush. He stomped a few paces and doubled over drawing in large breaths. After a moment, he screamed, so fiercely that every creature within a hundred yards fled. The branches of the nearby willows shook as the red robins took flight in every direction. He paused only to choke on the air his lungs drank greedily, and then bawled until he fell to his knees, sinking in to the lush green grass of the quaint cotton field.

This was his place of refuge. This was where he fled to find solace in times of trouble. It was the place he discovered when he lost both parents. It was the place he hid from the bullies, and it was the place where he had met Katrina Darringer, the girl he thought he would one day marry and grow old with. Talon squinted at the charming allure of the cotton field, but the pastoral scenery with its kaleidoscope of colours and flowers could not console him today. He doubted anything would every console him again.

He bounced to his feet wanting to move, wanting release, wanting some way to extinguish the hot coals that burned inside his core. He strode towards the centre of the field his favourite spot, his soul reaching out for some semblance of familiarity, or comfort.

He reached the spot where he and Kat had spent endless hours together forgetting the world. It was a beautiful point at the top of the shallow embankment overlooking the Hexon River. At night, it was the perfect place to nest while searching the stars. He kicked violently at a clump of blooming hyacinths, her favourite flower, and sent their violet petals streaming through the air in all directions. The movement, a vigorous affair which almost tipped him over, lifted several nearby cotton bolls into the air creating an ethereal shower of white fluff.

'Tal!' Kat's voice came from the trees.

His brows furrowed and, without turning around, he began marching across the cotton field ruffling more bolls in his destructive gate.

'Talon. Stop!' his pursuer screamed.

He ignored her clicking his tongue loudly.

Because of the waves of red-hot heat radiating off him, he half expected to set the entire field ablaze through touch alone. He stalked away from her through the field but she glided after him like a ghost in her white full length sun dress.

She caught up with him and yanked him around.

'Let go of me!' he barked, ripping his shoulder free.

She recoiled. 'What's wrong with you?'

'What's wrong with me?' He chuckled and shook his head.

She reached out to him once more, but thought better of it. Talon caught a whiff of her. She always smelled of freshly blossomed lavender.

'Please talk to me,' she said.

'Now you want to talk?' he said. 'We had months to talk.'

She cast her head down and cupped her hands in front of her.

'I'm sorry Tal,' she said. She rubbed the middle of his back.

'Don't touch me!' he hissed slapping her hand away. She withdrew and held her hands against her chest, shoulders arched.

'Did Dane do that?' she asked pointing at his left eye and bleeding nose.

'Leave me alone,' Talon said. 'Just leave, isn't that what you are planning to do, so go ahead and do it and leave me out of it.'

He glanced at her. She was crying. He hated how beautiful she looked in the fading crimson glow of the sunset.

'I should have told you I was getting married. There are no excuses. I just...' Kat paused. A bird squawked in the distance. 'I love him. I'm in love with him.'

'I don't want to hear this!' Talon shouted at her. 'PLEASE. PLEASE!'

He was crying now too. *Damnit!*

Her beige frock complimented her olive skin. He took one last look at her, the woman of his dreams, and then turned around wiping away his tears.

'I didn't mean to hurt you Tal,' she said. 'You know I lo..'

'Don't you dare say it. Don't you dare.'

She obeyed and they stood there in silence.

He roared.

'Forgive me?' she asked.

'No,' he said.

She was taken aback. The silence returned. The light faded into an array of pink and orange. The birds sang happily, some soaring lazily in the clear blue start-of-autumn skies.

'W-why not?' she asked. She sniffed.

'What are we Kat?'

'What do you mean?'

'What are we to one another?'

'Friends! Best friends!' she said.

'Friends…' he echoed.

'I can't imagine my life, my wedding without you.' She said. 'I demanded that you be my guest of honour. You and your M'ma. And we're going to have the wedding here in Shepard's Field, like I always dreamed.'

'Friends…' he whispered.

'Tal….'

'I can't be your friend,' Talon said. He strode past her.

She grabbed his arm. 'Why not?'

'BECAUSE KAT!' he yelled. 'Because, you were supposed to…. We were…. I just can't.'

'Oh, here we go again. Tal runs away as usual,' she shouted after him. She frowned at his back.

Talon's face was red and his mouth foamed, but his eyes were filled with tears.

'What happened to your dream of being a knight like your father? At least I am following my dreams,'

'I guess we were never friends at all Kat,' Talon hissed. 'If we were I would have known you were a shallow harlot ready to marry the first person with money or a title. Should've known a normal guy wouldn't stand a change with Princess Kitty Kat!'

Kat slapped him several times, 'DON'T… CALL… ME… THAT!'

Talon pushed her away.

'COWARD,' she said. Talon's eyes widened in surprise. It felt as though a knife had slowly slipped into the centre of his heart and Kat was the one wielding the weapon. He doubled over mouth wide with disgust.

'Talon,' Kat said. 'No, Talon, I'm sorry. TALON! I'M SORRY!'

But it was too late. He disappeared into the trees. He and Kat were no more. His dreams of marrying her were no more. And the cotton field… his place of solace. Well he had no place of solace.

2

THE LETTER

'KAT!' Talon shrieked.
He thrashed about in the darkness.
'Easy!' said the deep voice.
'I – I c-can't...' Talon gasped for air, 'Move. I can't move!'
'Stop you goat sack of a fool!'

The throbbing in Talon's belly gave way and with it came torrents of aguish. First the memory of it, sweltering in his middle, and deep within his skull, then the aching bones, and the stinging muscles and joints. His skin was on fire, to the point that sweat rained off him soaking through the blankets wrapped tightly around him.

There was a dim fire nearby, small, controlled, crackling warmly an arm's length away, but to Talon it felt like a conflagration. He howled as best as his raw throat would allow.

The sweet smell of burning pine filled his nostrils. Talon rolled over and threw up. He lay on his face in the dirt and vomit. He was hoisted up and set against a rock by a slender man.

Talon gasped for air, but every inhale rumbled smouldering stones inside his chest. His heart pounded heavily and his ears rang.

'Where, where a-am I?' Talon breathed.

'Sleep boy,' a man said. 'You need time to heal so stop waking up until you are ready.'

'W-wh-who are you?'

He tried to scream but is sounded more like a yelp.

The man placed his hand on Talon's head. 'I said SLEEP!'

He clicked his tongue and rolled back his head.

'No need for all that Telmache,' said the plump woman in her late thirties.

Her hair was tied back untidily so that stray strands fell across her round face. She disappeared into the backroom of her creaky shop.

The group of girls in front of him giggled. One of the girls dared to look back. When he caught her eye she quickly turned back to the rest. This triggered another round of giggles.

Talon shook his head.

'Here you are ladies,' Mrs Price said. She carefully lay an assortment of five dresses on the counter.

One of the girls, grabbed the dresses, and in unison they thanked her.

She smiled her warmest smile at them.

'Ah, Telmache what will we do with you?' Mrs Price said.

'I'm here for my M'ma's dress please and, and the gift… for you know who?' Talon asked.

'Hello Mrs Price. How are you Mrs Price? Me? I'm well, thank you Talon. And you? Oh, not too bad Mrs Price. Did you see that group of gorgeous girls in here a moment ago Mrs Price?' the woman said.

Talon blinked at her.

'Fine,' she said. Her voice came muffled from the backroom. 'You tell that M'ma of yours she owes me money.'

Mrs Price's daughter Peyton chuckled.

Talon scowled at her. She was four years older than him. Like her mother she had bright sky-blue eyes and a round face. Her hair was the same chocolate brown as her mother's. Most of the village boys worshiped the ground on which Peyton walked, but instead of indulging the attention she mostly kept to herself.

'Oh come on Talon,' she said. 'You've got to admit mummy is funny.'

Talon shrugged.

'And you tell her… you say, no paying with tinctures,' Mrs Price shouted from the backroom.

'Okay,' Talon shouted back.

She rummaged loudly in the back, 'Now where did I put it?'

'Heard you Kat's guest of honour?' Peyton asked. She had a thick pin clenched between her rosy lips. 'Taaallooon.'

He shook his head.

'Am I that distracting?' she asked her cheeks turning pink.

'What? No. Yes,' Talon said.

'Thank you,' she said. 'I think you are the first boy to just be honest about it.'

He gulped and attempted an awkward smile.

'I keep hearing how lucky you are to be her friend, but if I am honest I think she is lucky to have you as her friend,' Peyton said. She winked at him.

'We're not friends,' Talon coughed. 'Anymore.'

'You're not?' Peyton asked. 'Why?'

'It's a long story,'

'Oooh, I see,' Peyton said. 'I'm sorry.'

Mrs Price reappeared flustered. She blew at a strand of hair that fell across her nose.

'Here you go.'

Talon tried to swipe the dress in its protective sheeting and the gift box, but the large women was deceptively dexterous. She grabbed his hand and held on tight.

'Tell me dear,' she smiled. 'Aren't you darling Kat's best friend? Her guest of honour?'

'Not anymore mummy,' Peyton said.

Talon tried to rip his hand free, but he failed.

'You sure?' she said. 'Gossip is that you are. We all seen it. How close the two of you are.'

'Were,' he replied.

'Pardon me?' Mrs Price said.

'We were close,' he repeated.

'Were?' She said with a raised eyebrow. 'Why?'

'That's what I asked mummy, now leave poor Talon alone. He has his reasons.'

'She...' Talon began.

The woman leaned forward.

'Doesn't matter,' he shouted, successfully ripping his hand free.

'Good day Mrs Price, Peyton,'

'Damn you Telmache,' Mrs Price shouted after him. 'That's why no one likes you!'

'I like him mummy,' Peyton said. 'Bye Talon!'

Talon slammed the shop door behind him. A wave of chatter hit him as he entered the crowded street. He stood on the porch of Mrs Price's shop. The rusted words above the door read: 'Mrs Price and Daughter's Furrier

Company'. His grandmother must have gotten Kat a prize fur like her own. Talon was sure she would be pleased with herself.

He entered the swarm of shoppers buzzing, excited about finalising their shopping ahead of the Fetching Ceremony. Talon wasn't sure what happened during a Fetching Ceremony, he was only sure that he was a guest of honour, and doubly sure that he was not going.

He edged through the crowd, of browns, and greys and blacks and blues. There was always energetic activity from the villagers as they went about their busy country lives. However, since the news of Kat's marriage spread across the kingdom, the place was abuzz. There were strangers from all around the kingdom here to witness the royal marriage. Rumour had it that the king would grace the village too. This had everyone excited, because the king had barely been seen since the queen died.

His middling village was a haphazard collection of ancient stone and wooden buildings cast in between the Hexon River to the North and the Hexon Forest to the west. Women of all sizes and shapes shuffled around in droves, in and out of Mrs Price's. Each more desperate than the next to find the perfect dress for the upcoming wedding. Talon hated to admit it, but Kat's wedding would be the greatest event in the small community. The village had only had one drapery, and only one furrier, which doubled as the jeweller and perfumery. Both shops attracted substantial crowds at all hours of the day, and well into the night. Mr. Thomasson owned the only haberdashery in the village: a rickety warehouse with wares as obsolete as its owner.

Talon passed the mouldy haberdashery, where men ranging from teenagers to pensioners queued outside the door. Poor Mr Thomasson barked orders at his young assistant to help the next customer, while he guided another equalled aged man in dusty old clothes into a seat on his porch, which he had converted into an impromptu barbershop. The old man's eyes widened as Mr Thomasson's shaky hands edged closer to his face. The other men, each had a stout lager in hand, causing the place to reek of beer and smoke. They clanked their thick mugs together and spilt the yellow liquid jovially as they talked amongst themselves. The animated conversation would temporarily cease as a young maiden sauntered by, every eye following her down the street before they continued in their enthusiastic fashion.

There seemed to be more children in the streets, playing silly games around the busy adults, who clicked their tongues angrily when they tripped over a small boy or girl. Talon had never seen the village packed to such capacity. He rounded the corner and bumped into someone.

'Hiya Tal,'

'Sam?' Talon said.

'Sorry 'bout that,' the boy said. 'Wasn't paying any mind where I was going.'

'No, its fine,' Talon said. 'What news?'

'They're hear Tal!' Sam said.

He was a few inches shorter than Talon. The scrawniest boy in his year. He jumped into the air and clicked his heels.

'Who are you talking about?' Talon said chuckling.

Talon followed Samuel's finger across the road. Two columns of infantry marched through the street at a brisk pace. They wore the royal uniform – a mauve shirt and pants underneath a golden breastplate topped off with a red cape bearing the golden phoenix insignia of the Royal Family.

'Talon Telmache!' a high-pitched voice rang out through the crowd.

Three girls emerged from the wave of shoppers. The girl leading the pack was Anya Lowen, Kat's self-appointed best friend.

'Not now Anya,' Talon said. He cast his head left and right.

'Nuh, nuh Telmache, you won't escape us this time.'

He made to leave to his right, but another group of girls turned the corner ambushing him. He was surrounded.

'What do you want?' Talon asked Anya. He scanned the unhappy faces of the mob.

'Why did she make *you* her guest of honour?' Anya asked.

'He's what?' Sam said. 'King be damned!'

'Not you too Sam,' Talon said. He clicked his tongue.

'Do you know what an honour it is?' Anya said. She tapped her foot on the cobblestone pavement, and poked a bony finger into Talon's chest.

'It's not that big a deal,' Talon said.

The girls gasped.

'Guest of honour at a royal wedding. Not an honour?' Anya grabbed his collar.

'Anya,' another girl said.

Anya ignored her. She scowled, her face only inches away from Talon's. He retreated as far against the grey-brown stone wall as was physically possible.

'Best leave ya to business,' Sam said, slipping away into the ocean of shoppers.

Talon opened his mouth to call after him.

'What are you all doing?' Kat said emerging from the crowd. 'Tal.'

'Get your bloodhounds off of me Kat,' He said.

'Anya! Leave him alone,' Kat said.

'But Katy he...'

'ANYA,' Kat shouted.

The girl let go of her vice grip, and in the same movement Talon slipped away.

'Tal, wait...,' Kat called after him. 'Can... we talk? TAL it's been months. Talk to me!'

Talon ignored her, cutting left then right as fast as he could against the current of villagers moving in the opposite direction to the village square. He and several other shoppers stopped suddenly to allow a grand carriage carved with gold and silver to pass. Nobles flooded into the village to celebrate Kat's wedding festivities. Behind the carriage two more columns of infantry marched, followed by a large giggle of girls, and then – enthusiastic groups of young men burdened with large jugs of golden liquid. As soon as the strange procession passed Talon continued.

Several streets away, he pushed open the red creaky wooden door cast against a cracked double-storey grey stone building with the skew chimney. Talon entered his home and was immediately bombarded with the stench of burnt meat, mint, jacarandas and something else he couldn't quite place.

He closed the door behind him and placed his grandmother's parcels on the crooked table by the door.

He stood in a large open area that led into the kitchen. The walls were filled with shelves and shelves of glass bottles of various sizes with the widest array of items contained in them, from the giant squid head that gave him nightmares as a child, to the most beautiful black rose.

As could be expected, a tiny woman stood over some pots and pans. Her straight white-grey hair tied in a neat bun save for a single stray strand that refused to be tamed.

'You get everything?' she asked without turning around. Clouds of cinnamon-scented smoke filled the room.

'Yeah,' He said. 'It's all over there. Any food M'ma? I'm starving.'

'Boy, you always starving,' she said. Without further protest, she opened the oven and pulled out honey cakes filled with warm cream. He slid into one of two chairs at the kitchen table. Talon was sure his M'ma could give Mr Borden a run for his money. He made to grab one of the cakes off the platter, but M'ma rapped his knuckles with her wooden spoon. She had flour stains smeared across her faded black apron which was decorated with strange shapes that once resembled trees.

'Now you can have them,' she said. As she slid the plate on the table before him.

'Saw Kat and her spies just now,' he said before stuffing half a honey cake into his mouth.

'How is dear Kat,' She asked.

He shrugged, mouth full.

'You two still fighting?'

'She called me a coward,' he said.

'Well stop acting like one,' He scowled at her and took another large bite. 'Y' kn' I don' like when' p'ple call me tha'.'

'Don' be a fool boy. People gonna call you whatever they gonna call you, but you can't let that get to you,'

'Why they always picking on me?' he asked.

'You easy pickings,' she said sitting down across from him. 'Tell her how you feel.'

He coughed and choked. She came around the table and slapped him hard on his back. 'Serves you right, stuffing your face like a starved pig. Anyway, it's not too late to tell her.'

'Tell her what?' he said.

'You love her,' she replied. 'Don't play coy with me boy.'

He opened his mouth. Stopped. He thought about what he wanted to say, but came up empty, closed his mouth and took another bite.

'You done with your apprenticeship for the day?'

'All the masters hate me,' Talon said. 'And I'm not good at anything. Do I look like a furrier or haberdasher te you?'

'You'll find something,' She said. 'I've seen you do amazing things when motivated.'

'I could...,' he paused, scanning her face cautiously. 'I could sign up with the royal army.'

'NO!'

'They're conscripting again, while they are here,' he argued.

'I SAID NO BOY!'

'And they're taking more boys than they do from our village as a wedding gift or something...'

'TALON,' She said standing waving her spoon threateningly.

'I want to be a knight!' he said standing as well.

'Over my dead body!' She threw her spoon at his head. He ducked just in time. 'Not one more of my family. Not a one! Now clean that up!'

She straightened her apron and returned to her pots. He retrieved her spoon begrudgingly and handed it to her.

'Now get ready for the Fetching Ceremony,' she said. Talon opened his mouth. 'Boy, I swear, if you argue with me....'

'I don't want to go,' He said.

'Too bad,' she said. 'Guest of honour is only excused if dead. Something I am happy to help with, if you not ready in an hour.'

'I'm seventeen,' he said putting as much distance between himself and her.

'What that got to do with anything?'

'I don't need your consent next year,'

'BOY!' she threw her spoon at him once again, but he ducked into the hall and into his room.

His clothes lay scattered across the floor with scrolls equally scattered across the floor. His prized possession sat on his bed – an ancient leather-bound book with gilded engravings depicting a knight and a horse. The faded letters read: *Tales of a Legendary Knight: The Story of Travers Cailyn*.

'And don't read those rubbish fairy tales!' His grandmother shouted from behind the door.

She knocked on it loudly and then disappeared. Talon found it scary how she always knew what he was thinking. He decided to keep the peace.

Talon ducked into the bathroom, he kicked the bucket across the floor, and then picked it up. He was red. He exited out through their backdoor into their small yard and passed the small stable which housed his father's giant white steed. The creature's bored eyes followed him across the yard to the well while it gnawed ostentatiously at a fresh bale of hay. He kept a suspicious eye on the horse. It had a bad habit of messing with him from when he was a small boy, but his grandmother had never believed him. He grew up, but the horse never grew out of the bad habit of taunting him. Talon could only fathom that the horse took great delight in his torture.

He pumped the clean water and tossed it into a washing tub next to the pump. The yard was concealed by stone walls so it made for privacy except for the horse. Once Talon filled the tub, he built a small fire under it and frequently tested the water. At last it was ready. He shed his clothes messily and stepped into the bath. The process took some time, leaving room for his mind to drift off to thoughts of Kat.

'Hey Thayer,'

The horse ignored him.

'What was dad like?'

Thayer continued to chew loudly.

'I bet he was dashing and brave,' Talon said. 'M'ma doesn't like talking about him, or mom. She was from Hexon, you know. And beautiful, at least that's what everyone says. The brave captain and the beautiful maiden. That was supposed to be Kat and I.'

The horse looked up at him.

'You think I have what it takes to be a knight, like my father right?'

Thayer paused a moment and looked at him, then trotted lazily back to his stall.

'Stupid horse!' Talon shouted.

'Talon!' his grandmother shouted. 'Don't make me drag you to the feast naked.'

He blushed as he prepared to get out of the bath. An idea struck him then. He paused a moment and blinked stupidly. Talon sprang out the tub, slid through their home, and dove into his room, his towel barely covering his bottom. He scanned his desk for a clean sheet of paper, but only found a half-torn sheet with a previous doodle drawn across it. However, his quill and some ink proved much easier to procure. He dug both out of his trunk which lay hidden under his bed.

Once he had all the materials he needed, he plopped into his wobbly chair. It groaned from old age. He stared at the empty page and thought about what he wanted to say. *I love you? No – that's stupid. But I do. Do I?* Time ran on and nothing came to him. It was his grandmother's shriek that yanked him back to reality.

'You goat!' She yelled. 'Why are you not ready?'

'Because,' he screamed back at her. He had it. The quill scribbled across the page and the minutes passed by quickly.

'TALON!'

'Just a minute,'

'BOY!' she thundered slamming the door wide.

'DONE!'

'With what?'

'A Letter,' he whispered to himself. He folded it carefully and smiled. 'Just a letter.'

3

The Fetching Ceremony

His M'ma shoved him out of the front door and closed it behind them.
 'Mister Talon Telmache and Lady Blithe Telmache,' a tall finely dressed man said outside their door. He wore the mauve servant's clothes with the golden phoenix sigil etched onto his left breast.

'Who's this?' Talon asked. He pulled at his too-short brown trousers exposing his dirty socks and fiddled with the front of his matching dinner cloak.

'Our driver,' Blithe said. 'Now get in, get in. We're running late thanks to you.'

Behind the man stood one of the most ornately decorated open top carriage Talon had ever seen. Not that he had seen many carriages at all in his life. Fine golden figures were carved into the polished oak wood which shone enough to reveal his shadow reflection in it.

His grandmother pushed him forwards. The driver opened the doors for them. Talon hopped up the stairs and the driver assisted his grandmother. She wore her fancy dinner gown, a dark velvet grey dress with a long train that ran behind her as she walked. Talon always imagined it an heirloom from her past when she used to live in the capital. Come to think of it, he was not too familiar with her past before she moved to look after him in the village where he was born. They took their seats on the red cushions as the driver climbed his steps to his seat. Four well-groomed horses waited patiently for instruction.

'All ready?' the driver asked.

'Yes dear,' Blithe said. The carriage driver nodded, then ushered the carriage forward with a command and a flick of the reigns.

The sun had begun to set casting short square shadows over the tall rooftops of the surrounding buildings. Many villagers and visitors moved in the same direction as them, everyone dressed in dinner gowns or dinner cloaks with a complete array of assorted colours. A cool breeze passed through Talon's dark mess of hair drawing his M'ma's attention to its state.

'Bless the king, look at your hair boy,' she said. She frantically tried to comb it with spit and her hands.

'Stop already,' Talon protested. 'It's fine.'

'Fine my boot,' she said combing.

'Where are we going anyway?'

'Kat's house,' she replied.

'W-why?' he asked. He stuck his hand into his cloak pocket and felt for the letter he had placed there.

'That's how a Fetching Ceremony works boy. The fetch in fetching.'

Talon blinked at her.

'Well, it's all very 'mazing how it started,' she said. 'Was that a man could marry a woman just by kidnapping her. Jealous lads would steal a girl right before her marriage day and legally marry her so that the would-be groom couldn't do it. That obvious caused a fuss, so was that they added the fetching ceremony to the wedding.'

'But what happens? He asked.

'The boy. Well the man – he comes to the girl's house and asks for the girl's hand in front of her family. If she denies him, he is legally obligated to leave her alone, but if she says yes. Well, if she says yes, she leaves with him to get married, or that's how it went in the old days. Nowadays the couple form a procession where they ride around in their village or town for their folk to acknowledge their union, and it all ends with a feast.'

'So why are *we* going to Kat's house?'

'Guest of honour gets to witness everything. Usually they ride with the bride and her family too, but royal weddings are a little different.'

'We're 'ere your ladyship,' the driver announced.

His grandmother giggled at that. A sound Talon had never heard coming from her lips.

'Oh, I am no lady,' she said.

'I bet your ladyship,' he said winking.

They stopped three carriages down from Kat's front door. As soon as they arrived, a tall muscular young man, only a few years older than Talon, stood up from his seat on his even more ornately decorated carriage. A golden phoenix spreading its wings sat perched on each corner. He wore a fine mauve shirt, with matching robe, and on his head of fine blonde hair sat a giant opulent crown. The jewels of which reflected sunlight in all directions sparkling in the soft light.

'Look, it's Prince Calren,' Blithe gasped. 'Look how handsome he looks!'

Talon sulked silently.

The prince jumped from the carriage and strode to Kat's front door and knocked. The sizeable crowd assembled all around them cheered and applauded loudly then fell silent as one.

The second carriage, also finely decorated, held only one woman dressed in the most extravagant strapless canary yellow gown. She had the same colour light blonde hair as Prince Calren, and wore a crown matching that of the prince. She was the Princess Maya, Prince Calren's mother, and the sister of King Warrick.

The crowd cheered loudly. Talon stretched in his seat to see why. Kat's door opened. Kat emerged from the shadows wearing a white gown and white slippers with every inch of the dress etched in gold and silver so that it glowed in the light. Her light golden-brown curls were tied into tiers on her head. The gown was strapless and fit snug so that it revealed her ample bosom and melded well with her curves. She was radiant.

'Isn't she the most beautiful thing you have ever seen Tal?' his grandmother asked.

He didn't answer. Nothing else existed in that moment but Kat, amazing, beautiful Kat.

Halon and Nyclementia Darringer emerged from behind Kat. The crowd was still cheering wildly. In a smooth motion, the prince fell to one of his knees and begin to speak. Kat nodded in response to the question he asked her and the crowd erupted with deafening cheers and applause. The prince stood up and turned to Halon and asked something, and he too nodded. Kat's father was a tough man. Hard and cold, except to his two girls. He was also the mayor of Hexon Falls. The man had no love for anyone in the village least of all Talon, but he had less love for any boy who showed affection to his daughter, but when he nodded his approval to Prince Calren, he did so with tears in his eyes. The crowd ate it all up. Lastly, Prince Calren took Nycie Darringer's hand and kissed it and bowed, and again said something. Nycie nodded and Prince Calren proceeded to kiss her on each cheek to wild applause from the crowd. The Prince extended his arm to Kat, who interlocked hers with his, and the couple began walking to the carriage together.

Prince Calren, ripped Kat off her feet. The audience gasped as one to her screams, but all laughed and applauded when he placed her safely on their carriage. He jumped up after her and smiled a toothy grin to his subjects. Kat stood at his side waving and beaming at her fellow villagers. She was no longer just a villager, she was to be a princess and potentially the future queen.

Kat turned and caught Talon's eye. She smiled even more widely at his presence and waved frantically at him. He raised his hand slowly. Blithe smacked him at the back of his head. He waved back as enthusiastically as he could. His free hand remained in his cloak pocket clutching his letter tightly.

A flock of birds passed overhead chirping and singing loudly in the fading scarlet skies, drizzled with smudges of magenta and marigold against a sea of blue. The entire scene was a cascading shower of kaleidoscopic colour in every direction. Everyone was smiling and laughing and cheering the couple – all except Talon, who felt waves of loss flowing through him.

Talon blinked. The carriages began moving. Halon and Nyclemntia had joined Princess Maya in her carriage. The procession began to weave through the streets of Hexon Falls and everywhere they turned there were people with baskets filled with flower petals which they tossed at the carriages and cheered. Talon thought he saw Dane and his cronies all dressed up, but he turned to see again and they were gone, lost in the endless ocean of smiling faces. They turned the corner and were once again greeted with a roar of applause. Kat and Prince Calren were standing as their carriage moved forward. They waved in every direction beaming, but occasionally took a moment to steal a glance at one another.

Finally, the procession exited the town square which was complete chaos to navigate, because everyone swarmed, and pushing frantically to get a closer look at the royal couple. All the screaming gave Talon a head-splitting headache and for some reason his stomach kept cartwheeling. His M'ma was one of the people who applauded the loudest. She even occasionally whistled.

He glanced down at the crowd and saw Mrs Price and her daughter Peyton, donning a plum lace gown. He only caught her eyes for a moment. She winked at him and then she was gone. They drove down a dirt road known as Shepard's Lane, until they entered an enormous field encircled by the Hexon Forest. This field was known as Shepard's Field, aptly named because of the many sheep kept by Lord Reginald of the Hexon Family. Most all the lands for miles in all directions belonged to them.

A giant tent had been erected in the middle of the field. It was nearly four times larger than the town square. Symmetrical flame torches perched atop towering logs formed a long driveway that lead toward the monolithic tent. The carriages stopped in front of the main entrance. An army of servants approached them to help them off the carriages and to their table, a long table atop a makeshift wooden platform. Talon was seated at the end of the table, then his grandmother, then Nyclementia, then Kat, then Prince Calren, then Halon, then Princess Maya.

The tent was unlike anything Talon could have dreamed of. Thick wooden poles rose multiple storeys above the ground standing taller than the tallest pine tree in the Hexon Forest. These poles were strategically placed so that the tent canopies rose and fell in the patterns they were erected. Chandeliers made up of lilac, rose and turquoise jewels hung every few meters, Large torches were placed along the outer parameter with the walls of the tent rolled up so that fresh air drafted through the place. The moon, the torches and the jewel chandeliers together created an ephemeral feel to the place. Vibrant lilac, rose and turquoise shapes danceed on the roof and floor of the tent. Large circular tables were scattered throughout the hall, with pristine cutlery places at each table.

A large gong sounded, and then all the nobles were ushered in and seated at the best tables in the front of the enormous makeshift hall. As this was happening, a large orchestra to the right of the head table began to play melodic tunes the like of which Talon had never heard before. The sounds were serenading and sweet and gave him a sense of calm and ease.

Again, the gong sounded and the villagers and foreign guests began to trickle into the tent slowly group by group, each led by an usher or two.

'Hiya Tal,' Kat said. She had snuck behind him while he was marvelling at the majesty of the hall.

'Hi Kat,' He said standing. His hand automatically searched for the letter in his pocket. 'I wanted to tell you something, but couldn't find the w-words, so I w.'

'Oh Tal, this is Prince Calren,' she said cutting him off. The prince had just joined him. His smile was overwhelming. He swept back his smooth hair and extended a muscular arm.

Talon looked at the hand. Kat bit her lip. He saw that. That was what she did when she was nervous. She was afraid he would make a scene. He wouldn't give her the satisfaction, but he wouldn't shake Calren's hand either. Instead, he bowed deeply.

'Your Royal Highness,' Talon said.

Prince Calren laughed. Talon stood up and was swept up in a bear hug.

'No royal highness here Tal,' the prince said. 'Only friends. Kat has told me all about you. In fact, she can't stop speaking about you and what a great friend you have been to her. Thank you for being that to her Talon. I sincerely hope that we could have the same relationship one day, and that means you have an open invitation always to our home, always.'

'Your home?' Talon sighed after being released.

'In Terron Castle of course. Trina moves in after the wedding.'

'Trina?' Talon said looking at Kat.

'Sorry, Kat,' he said. 'She's my Trina, your Kat.'

'What were you saying Talon,' Kat asked.

He stared at the excited couple for a moment and then cleared his throat, 'I wrote you a letter.'

'A letter? Like when we were jammies?' she said chuckling. 'Tal, that is darling of you.'

He took it out. It was scrunched up, but he held it out to her. Prince Calren eyed it.

She took it, leaned forward and kissed Talon on his cheek. He hugged her tightly.

'Thank you for being here Tal,' she whispered in his ear. 'Really. It means more to me to have you here than to have any other person in the world here. You've made my night.'

'LADIES AND GENTLEMEN,' a large announcement rang across the room. 'PLEASE TAKE YOUR SEATS, THE FESTIVITIES ARE ABOUT TO BEGIN.'

Talon let go of her.

'Tal, why are you crying?'

'I don't...'

'Trina darling,' Prince Calren called her from her seat. Kat returned to her seat, but kept glancing back at Talon.

The hall fell to a deathly silence so that the crickets could be heard croaking away. In the distance a lamb bleated audibly, to which the audience chuckled.

'IT IS TIME AN HONOURED A TRADITION, THAT BOTH THE PATRIARCHS OF THE RESPECTIVE HOUSES TO BE JOINED SHOULD SPEAK...' the announcer said.

'Talon,' his grandmother said. 'What's the matter?'

'THE PATRIARCH OF HOUSE RENNER COULD NOT MAKE IT, SO WE WILL HEAR FROM OUR BELOVED PRINCESS MAYA INSTEAD ON BEHALF OF THE FAMILY...'

The audience applauded loudly.

'Nothing,'

'Nothing? You look's if you seen a ghost and it cut out your tongue,'

'What time does this end?' Talon asked.

'End? It's just started,'

'I'm not feeling good,' he said. 'I don't think I can watch this.'

'Hang in there,' she said. 'I will give you something.'

'LORDS AND LADIES, THE HUMBLE FOLK OF HEXON, AND MR. AND MRS. DARRINGER THANK YOU FOR HAVING US IN YOUR BEAUTIFUL VILLAGE,' said Princess Maya in a sonorous songful voice. 'WE ARE CONGREGATED HERE THIS EVENING TO CELEBRATE

THE UNION OF OUR TWO HOUSES, THE LOVE BETWEEN OUR TWO DARLING CHILDREN, AND THEIR MARRIAGE – LONG MAY IT LAST.'

'LONG MAY IT LAST,' the large crowd echoed. Almost everyone had found a seat at some or other table. And all eyes were on them. Talon imagined how strange he must seem to be at the table. Everyone knew it was only by Kat's insistence. The thought boiled his ears and made his brow sweat. He grew paler and more clammy every time a set of disapproving eyes glanced over him.

'WE WILL NOW RAISE OUR GLASSES IN A TOAST TO THE COUPLE AND GRANT THEM OUR BLESSINGS,' Princess Maya announced.

The army of servants went to work filling the tall, thin glasses on each table. Talon's glass was already charged with a clear bubbling liquid, that smelled of peaches. Talon undid his top button, but noticing his M'ma's eyes on him, stopped and tried to force a smile at her. She returned his smile with a frown.

'TYPICALLY THE TWO FATHERS WOULD MAKE SUCH A SPEECH AT THE FETCHING CEREMONY, BUT ALAS PRINCE CALREN'S FATHER IS NO LONGER WITH US AND HIS BELOVED UNCLE THE KING, COULD NOT MAKE THE CEREMONY,' Princess Maya pointed to the empty seat, next to her. 'HOWEVER, I SHALL SPEAK ON BEHALF OF MY SON...'

'You fool, you look horrible,' His M'ma said poking him in the chest with her finger. 'We'll find an opportunity to excuse ourselves early, and make our leave politely mind you. Wouldn't want these royal folk thinking we were raised by squirrels.'

He nodded.

'You hold it together now 'til then,' she said.

He nodded again, wiping his brow with his sleeve. The crowd burst into cheers and applause. His M'ma turned back to face their hosts and joined in, clapping as loudly as she could muster. Halon Darringer, stood up as Princess Maya sat down.

Silence fell again.

'YA ALL KNOW ME,' he said. 'CEPT THOSE THAT DON' I GUESS.'

The crowd chuckled, some clapped.

'MY BABY GIRL'S DREAMS BE COMING TRUE. SHE FOUND A WORTHY MAN – A LEADER, SOPHISTICATE AND SUCH.' As he spoke his walrus tusk of a moustache bounce up and down.

The crowd interjected with a peel of laughter. He waited for silence.

'IT WAS WORRISOME AT TIMES. YA KNOW THE COMPANY SHE KEPT,' Halon Darringer said looking down the table at Talon, who gulped audibly.

'Daddy!' Kat shouted.

'BUT MY BABY IS SMART AS SHE IS BEAUTIFUL, AND BY THE KING'S GRACE IS SHE NOT BEAUTIFUL?'

The crowd burst into applause. Wolf whistles and cheers rose through the tent. Kat's cheeks turned a peachy rose.

'AN' SO IT IS ME PLEASURE TE WELCOME INTO OUR FAMILY CALREN. A SON-IN-LAW WE ARE PROUD TE HAVE. TE PRINCE CALREN, WELCOME SON!'

The applause reached a record high. Nothing else could be heard except the clapping of hands and stomping of feet.

Prince Calren stood up, and all went silent again. He was well-built and tall with broad shoulders, chest, and arms. His skin seemed to glow the way Kat's did as if they were of a different species.

He raised his glass and said, 'YOU ALL HONOUR ME, BUT NONE CAN HONOUR THE WAY THAT KATRINA HAS BY ACCEPTING MY PROPOSAL. THERE IS NO WOMAN IN OUR KINGDOM, MORE CARING, PASSIONATE, BEAUTIFUL… OR FIERCE!'

The crowd chuckled in unison.

'HER OLDEST FRIEND TALON KNOWS WHAT I AM TALKING ABOUT,' He rose his glass toward Talon, whose eyes went wide. He dropped his grass on the table, picked it up and gulped loudly. Kat turned to him shrugged her shoulders. 'TALON, BROTHER, I WANT TO THANK YOU FOR TAKING SUCH GOOD CARE OF THIS BEAUTY FOR ME. SHE TOLD ME THAT YOU WERE A GREAT FRIEND TO HER ALL OF HER LIFE, AND I ONLY HOPE THAT YOU WILL CONTINUE TO BE SUCH A FRIEND, NOT ONLY TO HER BUT TO ME. YOU ALWAYS HAVE FRIENDS IN US. TO TALON.'

There was a faint mumble and no one clapped. Kat stood and began clapping as did Calren, and so reluctantly the rest of the crowd joined, but stopped as soon as Kat sat down.

'AND TO MY FUTURE PARENTS-IN-LAW…' Prince Calren said.

The crowd applauded and roared cheers of approval at his words.

'That was just rude,' Blithe said. 'You never mind these mannerless goat sacks all of 'em.'

'I'm so sorry Tal,' Kat shouted down the table.

'AND SO ON THAT NOTE, ENOUGH TALKING, LET'S EAT AND DANCE THE NIGHT AWAY!' Prince Calren finished. 'CHEERS!'

Prince Calren sat down and shrugged his shoulders. Halon Darringer smirked at Talon.

Calren clinked his glass with everyone at the table, walking to Talon as well who stood as he approached. Talon fumbled for his glass and raised it to Calren's. They smiled at one another, and then Talon was clinking his glass with the others at his table. He and Kat stood opposite each other, clinked their glasses, and then she hugged him.

'Forget them Tal,' she said.

'Sorry Tal,' Prince Calren said.'

He put on his best smile, hoping she was too distracted to notice he didn't mean it. They returned to their seats and were served the finest assortments of food Talon had seen. Roast pig and roast chicken, ornately decorated with vegetables and salads and cheeses. The courses kept coming, and although it all smelled exceptional, Talon had lost his appetite. He sipped on the bubbling elixir and prayed for the night to pass so that he could be alone. Not a single soul wasn't enjoying the festivities. Random groups would jump up occasionally and dance to the music played by the orchestra in the corner. The music's volume was perfect for the setting, loud enough to be heard over the din, but not too loud as to drown out what your neighbours were saying.

The mood was electric. In every corner of the room well-dressed people, lords, ladies and townsfolk chattered or chuckled. Their hearty spirits fueled by the sweet fruity tang of ferment which filled the room.

It was an unbearable affair for Talon, but the final stroke was hearing Kat's laugh, his laugh, coming from the makeshift dancefloor where Prince Calren swung her around in his arms felicitously. He used to be the only one who could make her laugh in her deep rumbling way always followed by streaking tears of joy. She threw her head back with laughter, holding on tightly to Prince Calren's waist. He had whispered something in her ear and cast a charming grin at her.

Without saying a word, Talon rose from his seat. He slid down the steps and strode towards the nearest exit thankful for the distraction the festivities provided. He was clear, with only a few steps away from the entrance flap, light from the full moon flooding into the tent, when he felt a soft hand grab his own.

'Where do you think you are going, Tal?' Kat laughed. 'You owe me a dance.'

'I don't feel well Kat,' he said, pulling his hand free and making for the tent flap.

'Why are you always walking away from me,'

He paused, 'What do you want from me, Kat?'

'I want to dance with my best friend – like we used to at the town dances,'

'I can't,'

'Can't what? Dance?' she teased. 'I know.'

Without a word, he turned away from her.

'Talon, where are you going?'

But he was gone, running away from that majestic tent, running away from Shepard's field, running away from her!

4

THE COWARD

A rooster crowed.
    Talon woke with a start sweating. For a second he forgot who he was, where he lived and what had happened the previous night. Thin streaks of light cut through his window illuminating dancing dust swirling in the air around him.

He sat up on his bed and wiped the sweat from his brow. The rooster crowed again.

Talon glanced out of his room window onto the empty street. He looked up at the sun and realised it was halfway to its peak in the sky. *Mid-morning.* He made his way to the kitchen and found a piece of parchment next to his breakfast. The note read:

> *Helping Kat and the women with their dresses. Will change here. See you at the wedding.*
> *M'ma.*

He ate in silence, but couldn't finish his meal. He had no appetite.

Why are you always running away from me? Kat's words rung in the back of his mind. *Coward.*

She was going to marry Prince Calren in a few hours, and he wanted nothing to do with it. He yawned widely and stretched. He was still tired from tossing and turning all night.

He had made up his mind last night. Most people in the village hated him. Even his M'ma thought him a coward, just like Kat. They would all be better off without him. He would take what little coin he had saved and travel. Perhaps he would even lie about his age and sign up to the royal army. There was nothing left for him in Hexon Falls.

After breakfast, he packed his travel sack, and then he went out back to the workshop. Thayer chewed lazily at his hay as usual, dark eyes following Talon across the yard. Talon found what he was looking for, his father's sword – a sword of a knight of the royal army. A captain's jewel was etched on to the end of the hilt.

He wrapped the sheathed sword in a blanket and placed it in his sack. He closed the shed door behind him.

'I'm going to become a knight Thayer,' he said. 'I'm going to travel and find a conscription office and push myself.'

The horse continued chewing loudly, eyes fixed on him.

'I don't care what you or anyone else thinks,' he said. 'I c-can't be with Kat but I can be a soldier. M'ma can't stop me. I'm going to leave before she gets back, while everyone's at the wedding.'

Thayer grunted.

He made to leave, and the horse grunted again, kicking over his trough this time.

'What is it?' he said.

The horse trotted casually to its saddle hanging on the fence and nudged it with his nose.

'You want to come with?' Talon said. He beamed.

'Thought you didn't like me?'

Thayer neighed and turned its head away from him.

'Oh, you just want out, you stupid horse,' Talon said.

Thayer kicked a bucket at him splashing Talon with water.

'Damnit Thayer!' he shouted. 'Fine. I have one stop first.'

He put the saddle on the horse the way his father had showed him. He opened the side gate and led the horse into the street. Talon started off left, but the horse stopped. He tugged on the horses reigned but it wouldn't budge. It turned the other direction and yanked him along.

'Stop Thayer,' he said. 'Stupid horse. I need to drop something off at Kat's.'

Thayer stopped for a moment and then turned around and once again allowed Talon to lead him. Before they reached Kat's house, the town bells rang, announcing the wedding. *Perfect timing.*

It was past midday and the sun sweltered directly above them in an empty sky, devoid of clouds or a breeze. The air was silent, as dead as the empty village. Everyone would be at the wedding. He wondered if his M'ma or Kat would care that he wasn't there. Both of them would be furious. This made him feel better about leaving. The lazy clicking of Thayer's hooves was the only sound reverberating off the walls.

At Kat's house, two large weeds crept up along the wall to the balcony that led to Kat's window which looked out onto the street. He had used it his entire life to enter her room without her parents knowing. He tied Thayer's reigns to the fence and climbed up the knobbed weeds to Kat's balcony. Her room smelled of her – fresh lavender.

He withdrew a shimmering emerald necklace, on a white gold chain made with the finest craftsmanship. This was all Talon had of his mother. This and a note which accompanied it. He unrolled the note that came with the necklace and read it.

To my beloved son, Talon. I leave you my prized jewel, given to me
by my soulmate, your father, for you to one day give to yours.
With my eternal love
Your mother.

She had written it while she was ill according to his M'ma. She died when he was too young to understand what was happening. He barely remembered her. He did remember her brown hair – long and beautiful and maybe her smile and her touch. He definitely felt her absence. There was no replacement for a parent, despite his M'ma having done her best. He missed his parents. He missed how safe his father would make him feel. He missed his father reading him Traver's heroic tales. A overwhelming emptiness pressed at his insides. This often happened if he thought about his parents too long.

A cat screeched in the alley pulling him out of his reverie. Talon wiped away a streak of tears and fell against the wall and closed his eyes for a moment. He imagined the life he could have had with Kat. A life now that would never be. The necklace dug a crevice into the palm of his hand from how hard he squeezed it. Perhaps if he could cling on to that a little longer, he could cling to his dream a little longer. He was unsure of how long he sat there sobbing quietly. Eventually, he got up, hung the necklace carefully on the balcony railing, and then rolled the note up and squeezed it in between the necklace and the railing. He made sure neither fell and then made his decent along the wall.

'Let's go Thayer,' he said.

The horse whined and they made for the village edge. He purposely took the path that would take him past the cotton field so that he could look at it one last time. When they reached the edge of the village a sonorous chorus of cheers and applause rang out from Shepard's Field. *All Hail the Princess Katrina Renner.*

Trumpets blasted loudly which brought on another chorus of cheers. A large rock rolled around in his stomach. It had sharp edges. He wiped away his tears. His Kat was no longer his. Maybe she was never his. Would things have been different if he had told her? Would she be his? Would it be him standing next to her?

The shade of the tree line broke the sweltering heat on the back of his head, as they entered the Hexon Forest on the southern-most part of Hexon Falls. The complete opposite end from Shepard's Field – a perfect escape route.

The earth shook violently so that Talon almost missed a step. Thayer neighed and reared.

'What was that?' Talon asked. 'Calm down boy.'

Again, the earth shook, more violently this time, followed by an explosion, and then screams.

'What's happening?'

A harrowing, painful wale of horn sounded, so loudly that it overpowered all sound, so that there was only that agonising cry as from some creature moaning in its last breath. When it finally stopped, the sound of squawking filled his ears. Every bird in the forest took panicked flight forming dark clouds of fear that swarmed in every direction.

Then came the screams again from Shepard's Field.

'What is that Thayer?' Talon asked. The hair on his arms stood on edge. His heart beat loudly in his chest. 'Huh old boy?'

Drums, deep and rhythmic beat sadistically and menacingly. A column of dark smog rose from Shepard's Field. The trumpet sounded again, but more sharply. There were shouts and then the sound of… *swords.*

The unmistakable clanking and clashing of steel on steel. The screams of dying men, of frightened women, the horrified cries of children. Thayer ripped his reigns loose from Talon's hand, and dashed in the direction of the commotion through the forest.

'Thayer!' Talon shouted.

Should I go? No. T-the royal army is here. They can handle it. Whatever it is.

A loud roar sounded from behind him. Talon turned and tripped backwards into the foliage. A large axe sunk into the tree trunk where a moment ago his head stood. He scurried backwards on the forest floor. Talon looked in the direction the axe came from, and about a hundred odd metres away, giants, draped in thick black furs brandishing spears and axes were descending upon him from every direction.

He shot up and ran as fast as his thin legs would carry him. Back into his village back into safety. He turned the first corner and ran into a wall of the same creatures, gigantic, menacing. He couldn't see a single face. Only black masks and where their eyes were meant to be, only dark orbs. The creatures in front of him charged him. He turned around, and a large crash rang behind him. Royal soldiers forming a shield wall had flanked the charging creatures, and cut them off. The street was splattered with dark drops of blood. Some landed on his own clothes. He remembered the others.

'More are coming,' he shouted.

A soldier heard him and repeated it. They finished off the last of the creatures, and turned to join Talon. As he predicted the rest of the warriors flooded around the corner and charged without fear. The soldiers shouted, 'For the King!' and charged as well. The forces crashed together violently. One royal soldier was impaled on a spear and lifted into the sky. More soldiers joined them.

One grabbed Talon, and twisted him around. 'Can you use this boy?'

Talon looked at the sword the man was thrusting into his hand. He shook his head. An axe sunk itself into the man's skull. He fell forward on top of Talon, a huge weight crashing down on him, enough to knock the air out of him. He squirmed out from under the man, and found the attackers and the royal army engaged in odd skirmishes.

'Get out of here boy,' Another soldier screamed. 'Get help! Do what you can! Protect your loved ones.'

'My loved...'

'Get out of here!'

'Kat! M'ma!' he shouted. He got to his feet. His right ear rang for some reason. He couldn't hear out of it properly for some reason. He ran up the street. The names escaped him. His thoughts were replaced with panic. He stopped for a moment, sweating, breathing, trying to thinking.

He jogged up the deserted roads towards the alleyway which would place him on Stable Lane, and from there he would find Baker's corner, cut through the town square, and head straight for Shepard's Field. A bearded man burst out of a building ahead. The sudden motion gave Talon a fright. He paused in his tracks. The man held two swords – one in each hand.

'Mr. Reginald?' Talon whispered.

The bearned man shot him a horrified look. Both swords rose wildly. His face was as white as his tangled beard. His one good eye, wide-open and alert took the measure of Talon, the other eye was sealed shut from his old military scar. He hesitated a moment, 'T-Talon Telmache?'

'What's going on Mr. Reg? –'

A crate crashed from around the corner. Both of them turned to look up the road for the source of the commotion. The sound of swords crashing together rang through the street.

'Quick boy,' Mr Reginald said, holding out a sword to Talon. 'Follow me and keep your wits about.'

The man began down the street at a brisk pace. Talon hesitated a moment. He looked up at the building Mr. Reginald had just appeared from. The golden letters on a wooden plaque above the door read: 'Jone's Armoury'.

'Com'on then ye fool,' Mr. Reginal said. 'We need te hel –'

A giant bear of a man appeared around the corner so quickly they had no time to react. It brougt down a hammer that smashed in to Mr. Reginald's shoulder sending him crumpling to the floor in a lame heap. The force of the blow ensured he slid across the cobbled streets at least a few feet with a river of his blood trailing after him. Another beast of a man appeard around the corner now too. They charged Talon.

He paused for a moment trying to process what was happening – what had just happened. It didn't make sense. The two monsters closed in on him but he dove to his right and crashed in to the cold stone wall just in time. He narrowly avoided an axe to the chest. However, his monstrous attackers were quick, and back on the assault, flowing seamlessly from their misstrike. Again, Talon was quick enough to avoid the second attack, barely rolling away in time. The axe scraped along the wall and then the pavement. Talon found his feet, jumped up, and dashed down the street.

He collided heavily with something, which made him plummet to the ground, disorientating him. The heavy drum of hooves reverberated around him, as he lay on the ground realing. A deep groan echoed in the street. It made Talon look up. He caught a glimpse of a horseman retracting his blade from one of the monsters that had attacked him.

'Ge' up lad, and arm yeself!' a voice called, yanking him upright.

'Wh-what's going on?' Talon stuttered.

'Are you daft?'

Talon blinked emptily at a tall soldier clad in his golden armour, whose blue-grey eyes pierced Talon's. The soldier held him by his collar so tightly that Talon had to stand on the tip of his toes to breath.

'Pick up your sword and fight for your life!' The solder said, throwing Talon backwards. 'Pick it up.'

Talon complied dizzily.

'Aye, now follow me and stay close. The rest of you battle formation.'

Talon looked around and found himself surrounded by soldiers dressed in the same fashion. 'What are those things?' he asked.

'Barbarians, lad, Barbarians,' the soldier said. He turned to his fellow soldiers and shouted, 'Move out!'

'Barbarians?' he exclaimed. The heavy sword trembled in his hands. Had swords always been this heavy?

They marched off in unison, feet stomping hard on the ground. Talon ambled after them as best as he could manage in his dishevelled state. Halfway down the street, a commotion erupted on their flank. The soldier closest to Talon stumbled sideways in to him sending him to the ground. The soldier, a young man not too much older than Talon, fell next to him.

A giant barbarian warrior ploughed through the soldiers with his axe. Several bodies dropped in his wake before the soldiers adjusted, drew their shields and counter-struck the attacker. The soldiers managed to lodge two shimmering blades with golden hilts in to the barbarian's torso. The giant's head fell at Talon's feet. He shimmied away across the cold cobbled road raising dust everywhere.

Beads of sweat dripped down his face. The side of his head throbbed painfully. His mouth was dry and his hands shook so wildly he could barely hold his sword straight now, let alone wield it against these fiends.

Another group of Barbarians decended on the the soldiers. They smashed into the walls and each other revving each other up. They roared as they reached the soldiers and crashed violently in to the shield wall like wild waves on rock. Talon's sword fell to the ground somewhere.

'HOLD THEM HERE!' the captain shouted. The soldiers shouted a response in unison. 'FOR KINGDOM!'

The captain thrust his sword in to the neck of a Barbarian who recoiled backwards as blood splayed over them all. Talon got on to his knees, and felt his stomach wrecht. He threw up and coughed to clear the bile in his throat, then he drew in air which stung on its way down.

Talon searched the area for his weapon, saw it lying a few feet away to his right and crawled to it. One or two screams sounded out behind him indicating the deaths of more soldiers. His eyes hovered on the blade a moment. He looked up the road and saw the Bakery up ahead. Shepard's Field was in that direction. *Kat!*

He left the sword, got to his feet, and bolted down the street as fast as he could. The captain howling in his direction before being cut off short of his curses. Only then did he notice he was crying. It was a strange senstation because he wasn't sad, just afraid to his bones. Parents told their children about barbarians to scare them and now the beasts of myth were buring his village to the ground. He stopped running a few roads away where the street was deserted. Everything was on fire. He placed his palms on his knees, leaning over and took deep breathes taking his bearings. He was close. Three streets away. But already he could hear the screaming and commotion from Shepard's Field.

He took a deep breath and jogged cautiously up the road toward the noise. He stopped where the cobbled road gave way to lush green grass. A hill obstructed his view, but the noise was loudest now. He was not sure what he would be walking in to. His eyes caught sight of a narrow path veering off toward the right, around the fenced off area in to clumps of trees. It was perfect. He ducked and ran as fast as he could bent over towards the narrow path along the fence and climbed the natural hill towards the trees. Once high enough he jumped over the fence with some difficulty, scraping his elbow on his way down.

He inspected the wound for a moment to make sure it wasn't too bad, and then he ran in to the trees, careful not to be seen from the field below. He reached the edge of the treeline and fell to his belly and crawled the rest of the way in the open to the edge of the hill. He couln't believe his eyes. Shepard's Field, a majestic flat piece of land atop a lush grassy area, was mostly ablaze, with women and children fleeing in every direction. The Kingsmen were involved in small skirmishes every few hundred metres as far as the eye could see. They engaged with the giant barbarian warriors, who wore their grotesque and twisted animal masks over their faces, some of wolves, some of wild boars, some of birdlike creatures. They all wore some or other fur and fought with tall swords, daggers, or a double sided axe that seemed to cut through people as easily as if it were cutting through a small clump of grass.

The monsters killed indiscriminanly. To his right, Talon observed with great horror, as a small boy accidently scampered in to the range of a particularly large Barbarian whose axe sliced the boy clean in two. The boy's mother screamed and cried at the top of her lungs running towards her boy's body, and was met with the same fate, chopped down from right shoulder to left hip. The Barbarian roared in victory, but a knight shot past, lifting the Warrior's head clean off of his head. As if resisting death, the headless body of the giant stood defiantly for a few second, before crashing down towards a group of shrieking maidens. One of the girls was too slow. The enormous, bloody carcass crashed on top of her middle sending her hurling to the ground. She screamed loudly while trying to worm herself out from under the sizeable mass, but her screams only attracted another Barbarian who silenced her for good.

Talon shut his eyes. He tried desperately to remove the image of a Barbarian axe being yanked out the young woman's head. However, the image stuck with him, seared to the back of his eyelids and every where he looked he saw that terrified expression frozen at the time of her death. He was shivering despite the heat beating down on them from the summer sun. Thick plumes of black smog concealed the fact that it was actually a beautiful day. He grew more and more anxious with every passing minute. *Where are you Kat?*

There was a large group of people congregated on the farthest part of the field. Talon could make out the red and gold of Kingsman, many on horses – knights who were with the group, but thick veils of smoke kept sweeping by in the wind obstructing his vision. There was nowhere else on the battlefield she could have been, unless she was already.…. *No! She's alive. She has to be alive!*

Talon slithered backwards to the treeline, got up and dusted himself off, and then made his way around Fletcher's field as quickly as he could keeping to the edge of the treeline. Sometimes he ran, sometimes he jogged and sometimes he sprinted, twisting slowly around the outside edge of the field in line with the large trees towering it.

Just before he reached the other side he stopped and dove behind a large maple tree's exposed roots to avoid being seen by a sizable group of barbarians. They appeared to be coming from within the forest. He peaked around the edge of the tree and spotted the first three Barbarians he had seen the entire day riding horses. The one in the centre stuck out the most. He was the only barbarian without a mask. He had an angular, pale face with dazzling grey eyes. He was good-looking. Handsome even. One would never say he was a Barbarian, but that he was built like one, if not perhaps slightly leaner. A large number of Barbarians rushed past them towards the battlefield, and these three trotted along leisurely chatting away about something in what Talon could only fathom was the Barbarian tongue. He twisted around the tree trunk on to the other side to follow the Barbarian's assault on Shepard's Field from his safe hiding place.

The Barbarians engaged the Kingsmen surrounding the large group of people. For a fleeting moment, a gap was created by all the fighting and through it, Talon caught a glimpse of a white dress. *Kat!* She was amongst the trapped citizens protected by the Kingsmen force. They had knights of the Kingdom as part of the force. He remembered stories of his father, and of his hero Travers Cailyn, both knights in the Royal Army. They defeated greater enemies than this Barbarian force. Surely these knights too would defend Kat. He jumped up and ran in to the field keeping as low as he could. He reached some carts and wagons used by the people who had set up the large tent.

His vision of the entire field was obscured by black smoke. The same smoke allowed him to approach the group of people, several hundred metres away. Barbarians and Kingsmen were engaged in combat on all sides. Both sides had victories and both sides had losses, but for every loss the Kingsmen suffered, the fight got worse, because they faced more and more enemies, until the last knight fell to a dagger thrust in to his side. His horse fought on for him until a large axe found its mark on the creatures neck sending horse and rider to the ground. They were defeated by sheer number.

The group of people they protected were mainly women and children, but in amongst them stood Prince Calren, dashing and fierce despite the dirt smeared across his face. He stood back to back with Kat, both of them wielding swords and seeming worse for wear. Her dress was torn so that her bare thigh was exposed. She had cuts and bruises all along her arms and a large gash across her cheek.

Talon wanted to run to her but his legs sunk in to the ground. He circled around the wagon and once again lay flat on his belly. He caught glimpses of Kat through gaps in the Barbarian ranks, between their legs, or where someone broke away from the group.

'No!' she yelled. The women and children screamed. Talon made to jump up, but hit his head against the underparts of the carriage where he lay in hiding. It throbbed while he lowered himself back to his belly to crawl out. He identified a group of stacked casks not more than twenty metres from the circle of people. He scanned the group of Barbarians to make sure no one was watching, and then sprinted as fast as he could for the casks.

'Don't you dare touch him,' Kat shouted.

A slap resonated throughout the field. Talon twisted around the casks. He searched the spot where he last saw Kat. His view of her was obscured by wide barbarians, but every so often he would catch a glimpse of her white dress.

A Barbarian shifted closer to his fellow warrior to whipsper in his ear, which gave Talon a clear view of Kat. She cupped the left-side of her face, but did not let it impede her efforts to tackle a particularly grizzly barbarian warrior who dragged the unconscious Prince Calren away by his blonde hair. The barbarians laughed as she struggled futily with the man nearly twice her height and thrice her width. He swatted at her lazily with his heavy arm as if swiping away at a pesky insect. They disappeared out of Talon's field of vision.

'You're the new princess of the worm men,' A smooth sighing voice said loudly. 'Soon to be queen of the worms.'

Talon couldn't see from the cask. He glanced around for an alternate hiding spot, but the only viable ones were too close to the Barbarians.

'What's it to you?' Kat huffed back. 'I demand that you let my husband go!'

Husband. The word pierced Talon. Kat was married.

'Let me be the first to congratulate you *princess*,' the man said sheepishly. Talon still couldn't see what was happening.

'S-st-STOP,' Kat screamed.

'There is no use struggling princess. That is a barbarian berzerker. The highest honour that can be bestowed on a barbarian warrior. You are lucky he likes you, or you would have already been dead,' the unmasked man said. The barbarians roared with laughter.

'Release my husband,'

'Release my brother,' the man replied. He sat lazily on his horse.

'W-what's your name?'

'It is of no consequence,' the man said.

'You speak well for a barbarian,' she replied.

'It disgusts me to speak this pathetic tongue, but it is beneficial,'

'We are not your enemies,' Kat said. 'Please…'

'Drag'a,' the man said.

The barbarians all roared in unison and hit their chests.

'What is that?' Kat cried.

'My name princess, my name,'

'Please release my husband. I beg you. Leave him and my people,' she said.

'Release your husband?' Drag'a said. The barbarians grunted. 'I cannot dishonour this warrior… I cannot tell him that. Your husband is his *nbral* – his conquest. He has won your husband as a slave fairly,' the smooth voiced Barbarian said. The Barbarians roared in agreement.

'Please,' Kat pleaded.

'I would princess, but I need your husband,'

'Please,' Kat exhaled.

'What if I took you instead?' he asked.

Kat remained silent. Talon imagined the stunned look on her face. He had seen it many times. A horse neighed. Flies swarmed over the open carcasses left on the battlefield. The smell of blood and flesh filled the air. The wet grass underneath him crunch as he shifted to catch a line of sight.

A strong breeze gave them repreive from the beating sun. Though its light was blocked, its heat beat down on them. He wiped his brow, and crawled to the opposite end of the stacked casks to see if he had a better angle from there. A short distance closer from that side stood a cage atop a four horse carriage, drawn by large horses with midnight black coats.

'No answer?...'

Talon glanced at the crowd. All eyes were on the speakers. So, as quick a he could, he dashed the few metres past the horses and dove under the carriage and rolled past over to the other side and then knelt against the large wooden wheel. The horses snorted loudly and stamped their feet.

'Y-yes, take me instead,' Kat said.

Talon gulped at the words he heard, but was distracted by what the Barbarian said next, because one of the bezerkers coughed something in their harsh language. The berzerker's shadow appeared around the edge of the carriage on Talon's side, just before he did. This gave Talon enough time to slip back under the carriage. The heavy boots trod past him toward the horses. The Barbarian spat instuctions at the horses who insanely fell silent. Then the boots returned the way they had come.

'Tempting,' Drag'a said. 'Your beauty is incomparable. I would have great pleasure breaking you, but I need the worm king to pay attention.'

Kat shook her head crying.

'who better than to take his only hier – the future king of the land.'

'If you took me, the king would listen – he likes me, and I am told that he doesn't like anyone,' Kat rambled.

'N-no Katy,' the voice of Kat's mother cried.

'Shhh now,' Talon's M'ma said. Nyclementia's sobbs were muffled. Talon peaked around the carriage and saw Kat's mother's head nestled in his M'ma's breasts as she consoled the women. Most of the crowd, clung to each other in the same fashion sobbing silently in to each other's shoulders.

A loud horn sounded in the distance in the direction of the village. One of the mounted barbarians barked a short instruction mobilising most of the Bezerkers who marched off quickly. Talon hoped it was help. Within a few strides the warriors disappeared behind the rolling walls of smog and ash.

Few of the barbarian warriors remained – too many, some bezerkers noticably taller than the others – too many to imagine doing anything, but the decrease in number provided Talon a clearer view of Kat and the barbarian leader. His long wavy black hair billowed in the wind and a matching pair of dark grey eyes cut through Kat's countenance.

Drag'a tucked a stray lock of Kat's golden curls behind her ear. While she closed her eyes and cringed at his touch.

'Behold the future queen of the worm men,' Drag'a said in his smooth sigh of a voice. He said something in the gutteral Barbarian tongue. It must have been funny, because all the barbarians chuckled, some snorting as they did.

Kat scowled at the barbarian.

'I admit princess – your offer appeals to me. I imagine laying with you while we travel. You won't like it at first. We *Vrolfolk* – barbarians – as you call us have a wilder nature, and just look at this body,' he said. He spanked Kat on the bum, then yanked her by the small of her back right against himself.

She slapped him audibly, dug her palms in to his chest and shoved him. He barely moved, but released her from his grip anyway. The Barbarians roared with mirth.

'What's so funny?' Kat said.

'They're laughing because they have never seen a barbarian war lord ask a woman's permission to touch her before,' he clicked his tongue and grinned. 'What do the worm men call a woman like you? There is a word...'

He turned to one of the mounted barbarians. The barbarian replied in the harsh dialect.

'Yes, Thank you Vrgraer, *goddess,*'

Kat winced and backed away as he edged forward toward her.

'She smells like wild flowers Vrgraer,' the Barbarian said.

The mounted man remained silent. The other horseman, drew out a whip in a quick fluid motion. He cracked it to their left, hitting a Barbarian warrior pestering another pretty maiden in a green dress at the edge of the group.

'Leave them alone!' Kat yelled.

'You heard the goddess,' Drag'a said. He nodded in the direction of their lecherous colleague. Two of his fellow warriors, grabbed each of his arms and dragged him away from the crowd. He wailed as they took turns cutting him with thick serrated blades made of yellow bone.

'Stop hurting him!' Kat pleaded. Stop hurting people. Just leave us alone.'

She beat against his chest, slapping him and punching him as fiercely as she could manage. The horde drew their weapons and growled fiercely. The crowd of hostaged wailed in response, some cringing in anticipation of their deaths. The handsome barbarian, their leader, raised his fist and the barbarian horde fell silent. Some snorted wildly under their animal masks, visibly uspet with the decision.

'Women,' the handsome Barbarian sighed.

The Barbarians grunted and snorted with laughter.

A long wail of the Barbarian horn sounded again. All the Barbarians raised their hands in victory. Some of the Barbarians made to take the hostages. One Barbarian, ripped a little girl from her mother, and took the girl over his shoulders. The girl shrieked arms outstretched toward her mother.

'Please don't do this – I am begging you,' Kat said grabbing Drag'a's collar. 'Don't.'

The Barbarian grabbed her again, and she didn't struggle, but turned her head away as he drew her in. He barked orders, and the horde fell silent. He spoke again, and the horseman with the whip cracked it at some of the warriors. They all protested until their leader gave a deep gutteral grunt. Kat's eyebrows rose at the sound emenating from him. He spoke once more and reluctantly, the large grizzly berzerker holding Calren dragged him towards the cage.

'No, no, no,' Kat repeated as she struggled against Drag'a's grip.

'Silence girl,' Vrgraer thundered from his horse. 'Respect our *Kgren*, Last Son of Bragar *Vrolgar Kgren*!'

'Vrgraer, she doesn't speak our tongue,' the handsome Barbarian said. 'Your words mean nothing.'

'You're Drag'a, Son of Bragar, Chieftain of the Bezoboar Hordes,' Kat said.

Drag'a looked at her with raised eyebrows and open mouth. 'Very impressive. Your people know me? You see Vrgraer, I am famous.'

'Your father,'

'Yes,' he spat. *'Him'*.

The bezerker dragging Calren reached the carriage, hoisted the prince up and threw him in to the cage. His limp body slapped agianst the back, his head hitting the metal bars and his leg twisting in the wrong direction.

Talon waited. The bezerker slammed the cage door closed, but he did not hear the chink of the lock. It was still open. He looked inside and saw the chiseled features serene, unaware. He looked up and caught Kat's eyes, and ducked. His heart racing. *She saw me! Did anyone else?* He placed his palms on the course wood of the carriage's side panel to stop his hands from shaking.

Drag'a issued more orders to his horde in the Barbarian tongue. The horseman with the whip, repeated them in a terrifying, grating voice that carried on the air. The sound made the hairs on the back of Talon's neck stand on end. The Barbarians mobilised in every direction as though the hostages weren't there. Drag'a still held Kat close to him. She crossed her arms to keep some space between them. Her white dress, however sullied from the battle, contrasted heavily with his thick black fur cloak and armour.

She turned away from him while he spoke and looked over at Talon again. He looked at her. *Help him,* she mouthed. She fought down the disgust she felt at the Drag'a's touch – a distraction to buy Talon time.

Talon recoiled backwards as if struck by a viper. Prince Calren had touched his hand softly through the rusty metal bars of the cage. 'Hel…'

The prince's hand went limp. He looked down at the prince, at Kat's husband, and not a single bone in his body wanted to help him. This was the man who had stolen Kat from him. If they took him away, perhaps….

He backed away from the carriage. He looked up forgetting that she was watching. He found her staring at him with those piercing tea-green eyes filled with tears. She blinked them away and whispered what looked like *please*.

He shook his head slowly, automatically as if he were being controlled by some inexpicable force. He angled left towards the large horses that would draw the carriage. This took him out of her sight, but he could never erase that look from his mind.

'TALON YOU COWAAAARRRRDDDDD!' she bellowed at the top of her lungs.

'Princess,' Drag'a said shocked. 'I thought we were getting on so well.'

'DON'T TOUCH ME,'

'Ah ah ah,'

'LET GO OF ME YOU PIG,'

'Talon the coward?' Drag'a said loudly. 'Come away from the cage.'

Talon froze.

'You think we don'y know you are there?' Drag'a said. 'This worm princess cares for you coward. Come out or I will kill her.'

'Run Tal, run,' Blithe screamed. A bezerker hit her with the back of his hand.

Talon stood up.

'Tell the worm king I swear on my father's name that he will never have an hier again, until he returns my brother to me,'

'What w-,' Kat began.

Drag'a slipped his sword into Kat's belly. She stared up at the barbarian and slowly went limp in his arms. The hostages cried out loud. Nyclementia screamed at the top of her lungs.

'Of course your corpse is a more effective message,' Drag'a said. The barbarians roared.

'Kat!' Talon shouted edging forward.

Drag'a looked at him and laughed. He looked at one of his bezerkers. 'Kill the coward.'

Kat fell to the grounded gasping for air, eyes wide.

The whip cracked harshly.

The grizzly Bezerker snorted then charged.

'TALON!' a voice shouted.

Kat was dead.

5

THE TWO ROADS

His life was over.

'RUN TAL!' his M'ma's voice echoed.

His body sprang back to action. Twisting around quickly, he sprinted away towards the trees about two hundred metres away. He slipped on the long grass but straightened and kept going. He sidestepped the first tree when the bark near his head exploded. The thick gleaming blade of a double-edge axe sunk violently in to the trunk at head level, scattering splinters everywhere, some in to Talon's left cheek. He tumbled over the roots of the next tree and crashed shoulder first in to the bottom of the trunk. He jumped up despite the sting in his shoulder, breathing heavily through gritted teeth. He twisted through the air as the edge of a dagger clipped his elbow with such force that it lift him off the ground.

He screamed as he crumpled on the ground. He kicked off doing his best to keep rolling. It was good that he did because the dagger swiped past his abdomen. The thrust of the blow sent the gigantic Berserker steaming past Talon. This gave him time to get to his feet and bolt away in the opposite direction. He wasn't sure where he was headed, but his head spun, his lungs burned, his elbow stung, his head throbbed and his heart pounded. He did not stop, but cut left ahead. He heard a whistling, and then his right shoulder propelled forward in to the nearest tree dragging him along with it. The dagger had clipped his shirt and the force carried him with it into a nearby tree.

He ripped himself free of the dagger caught in the tree. After stumbling a moment, he continued running for his life. After a minute, he broke through the treeline into a clearing. He didn't dare look back, but kept running. He didn't slow down, but kept his pace. The exertion was excruciating, but he kept running. He reached the next treeline and leaped behind the first tree, doubled over, and swallowed as much air as he could. He glanced out back over the field. The Berserker was halfway across, when the haunting moan of the Barbarian horn sounded again. The Berserker stopped, his thick chest rising and falling heavily. He eyed the treeline where Talon stood greedily. The horn sounded again.

Reluctantly, he turned and ran with the same intensity towards the horn. Within a few strides the warrior disappeared in the trees on the other side of the clearing and all was still again. The crickets who fell silent in the monster's presence, continued stridulating as if nothing had changed. Nature continued as normal, unconscious to Katrina Darringer's absence.

Talon ran as quick as he could back to the field, but he was too late. He only caught a glimpse of them loading Kat's pale body onto a cart. Her white dress was stained from her torso down. His grandmother and Nyclementia got into the cart and Anya, one of Kat's bridesmaids, climbed into the driver's seat and whipped the horses who sped off. The rest of the women and children ran off in all directions. Some heading back to the village, others to the field. *Where are all the men?*

He made it back to where Kat had been stabbed. A young maiden sobbed on the ground unable to move.

'Where, where are they taking her?'

'She's dead,' the maiden said.

'Where are they t-taking her, her body,' Talon asked.

'They just killed her,' the girl said.

'Where are the men,' Talon asked.

'All dead,' she said. 'They're all dead!'

He knelt and shook her as hard as he could.

'Where are they? We need them to help.'

She pointed.

'Thank you,' Talon said. He wouldn't be able to catch up to Kat's cart, but he would be able to get the men to help find out where they were taking her body – where they would bury her.

His vision blurred from the tears. He passed through some smog and on the other side he stood frozen once more. His stomach somersaulted. He fell to his knees. Dead, mangled, bloody bodies lay strewn across the lush green field – women, children, but mostly men, young and old. *They're all dead.*

A young girl with twin braids screaming in the middle of the field. She was bleeding from her head. Her mother crouched over a dead body not a few metres away crying and shaking the person in a desperate attempt to bring them back. He wanted to hold Kat that way. He wanted to hold her one last time.

Everywhere scattered groups of women searched for dead fathers, sons, brothers, husbands and lovers. Very few men were left. He couldn't see one standing and searching the field. *Are they all dead?*

Widowed women wailed. Everywhere just wailing. The forlorn sound drowned out anything else.

'COWARD!' someone shouted to his left. It was Mrs Price. 'He's dead because, b-because of you!'

'M-mummy th-that's not true,' Peyton cried. Her cerulean dress was torn by claw marks.

'Why is he still alive, and your d-darling father...' the older women cried into her daughter's shoulder.

'HE IS A COWARD,' Another woman said. 'I saw it with my own eyes!'

'N-no I'm not,' Talon stuttered.

'She asked you to help the prince. I saw it,' said someone else.

A bony woman slapped him across the face. The sound echoed and the force sent him rolling on his side. The other women ached for their turns. His back, the top of his head, his shoulder. The women surrounding him continued to slap him viciously. A nail sliced the side of his neck. He stood up with great difficultly, arms raised to defend his head. He tried to pull away but they gripped his shirt.

'P-PLEASE,' Talon pleaded.

'COWARD! COWARD!' they repeated.

Someone forced him away from the others, 'STOP!'

It was Peyton. She held her arms out in front of them. A tall elderly woman slapped her too. She crumpled and held on to the place where she was slapped.

'You defend this coward?' the tall women spat.

'Go Talon. Just leave,' Peyton shouted.

He nodded at her, got up and ran his cheeks stinging, and tears filling his eyes.

'DON' YE COME BACK 'ERE EVER!' someone shouted. The mob cheered.

He reached his burning village and meandered through the streets, unable to take a direct path because of the fire ravaging through the village. It consumed whole buildings at a time without discrimination.

Thick plumes of toxic smoke billowed high into the would-be blue sky. Young children and women ran from the wells loading water into buckets. They stumbled with their heavy loads and poured it pathetically over their homes. It was no use. Their attempts only enraged the inferno. They could barely stand five metres away from the fire without their skin boiling. Others watched their homes crumple into ash and dust crying.

COWARD. The thought sliced at him. He stopped, leaned against a brown moss-infested wall, the only not burning. He doubled over and gagged but nothing came up except for a sliver of bitter saliva. *It's my fault. I-I should've helped.*

COWARD.

'P-please help us mister,' a child called. He ignored the boy.

COWARD.

He didn't stop running until he found his travel sack where he had left it on the other end of the village. Thayer stood restlessly near his pack, kicking up dust as he did.

'You're alive,' he said to the horse.

Thayer nickered then turned and began walking on the path they would have followed a few hours ago.

'We can't come back Thayer. I can't,' he said.

The horse stopped a moment and looked back.

'S-s-she's dead,' He said. Tears streamed down his cheek stinging them from their bruises caused by the women. 'And it, it's my f-fault!'

The horse snorted loudly. It looked at him for a moment and then continued walking.

He sat on the ground crying for Kat, crying for his village, crying for all those that were lost, and crying for the end of his life as he knew it. He wasn't sure how long he sat there, but when he looked up there were no signs of the horse.

'Thayer!' he shouted. No replies. 'Y-you stupid horse!'

He thought he heard a distant grunt, he got up, wiped his face on his beige shirt sleeve and chased after the horse. The forest was dark, with only stray shots of bright light bursting through the canopy. The ground was cool under his boots and the dark dirt crunched softly under his feet as he walked briskly to catch up with the horse.

A breeze rustled through the trees after a few minutes. He could still smell the smoke from his village, and on his own clothes. The sound of insects croaking, buzzing and whistling was overwhelming in the forest. He was surrounded by an assortment of strange sounds. The birds took rapid flight in the trees to his right giving him a start.

'Thayer dammit!' he said, catching the horse. 'I'm the human. I say where we should go. You are the horse. You wait for me.'

Thayer flicked his head shaking his long white mane. He stood the same height as Talon, a tall horse as far as horses went. Talon knew he was a rare breed, which was almost exclusively used for the knight's service. Other people might notice that too. *We'll have to be careful.*

'My leg's hurt,' Talon said. 'Slow down so I can get on.'

Thayer disobeyed and continued walking. Talon secured his travel pack awkwardly to the horse's rear, and then tried to place his foot in the horse's stirrups. Thayer sped up to a trot and Talon tumbled over into the dirt.

'Fine,' Talon said, getting up and dusting himself off. 'I'll just walk.'

He could have sworn the sound coming from Thayer sounded like a chuckle. They broke free into the clearing of the cotton field. Talon walked automatically but his eyes were fixed on the devastation. The field was ablaze. Filled with black and white ash where there used to be green.

'What did they do,' Talon mouthed. Thayer continued walking. He paused to take in the cotton field. He and Kat's spot. The place he had fallen in love with her was destroyed, dead, like her. *I'll never see her again. I'll never see this place again.* Thayer neighed. He had already disappeared into the tree line on the other side of the clearing. Talon wiped away his tears, and went after the horse.

They continued walking several hours, until darkness threatened to envelope them. Talon was worried about finding a place to settle, but every spot he chose, Thayer would just continue walking. Talon sighed with great relief when the horse finally stopped near a tiny stream with soft trickling water. The shallow embankment of the river made for a perfect bed for horse and young man. Talon removed, his sack of gold, ten coins, his entire life-savings accumulated from the odd jobs he had assisted with around town, and those acquired as birthday gifts from his M'ma. He also removed his beloved book filled with Travers's adventures. Lastly, he pulled out a honey cake. He placed a blanket down on the grass and proceeded to make a small fire. It took him some time, all the while Thayer nickered and snorted with frustration at watching the pathetic attempts.

Night had already descended for about an hour before Talon got the fire going. He drank a few sips of water from the stream, as did Thayer, and then he retreated to his blanket, where he nibbled on the honey cake, counted his gold coins over and over, and read his favourite paragraphs from his book – paragraphs telling of how Travers had saved the queen from barbarians and how together they had survived the haunted mountains. *He saved the girl. I didn't.* The rest of the night Talon spent crying in silence. An owl hooted loudly above them. The forest canopy prevented him from seeing the stars. The dim orange light of the fire, turned to a cold red, just a few ember smouldering.

Thayer snored loudly, the crickets ratted away into the night and slowly, with great sadness, exhausted and spirit broken, Talon fell asleep.

Kat's body shook violently, ripping apart the stitches over her bare belly. Blood gushed out of the wound, and her mouth foamed, then she began vomiting out of the side of her mouth.

'Quick,' M'ma shouted. 'Turn her on her side, so it all comes out.'

'What's happening to her?' Nyclementia cried.

'Nycie, give me some room!' M'ma said.

The elderly women placed another damp cloth over Kat's stomach and muttered under her breath. With her other hand, she shoved two fingers down Kat's throat forcing her to throw up again.

The girl stopped convulsing after her stomach was emptied. She lay deathly still which made Nyclementia only wail louder, until Kat drew a deep breath, opened her eyes and passed out again.

'How long before we reach Terryn?'

'Please Blithe save her,' Nyclementia cried.

The wagon shook wildly on the uneven dirt road. All of them fell too hard.

'Dammit Anya,' Blithe shouted. 'You tryin' to kill us all?'

'I-I'm s-sorry,' Anya cried. 'I can't see anything. I've never driven before.'

The flaming torch perched on the end of the wagon only provided enough light to see a metre or two ahead.

'There, there, you're doing fine.' Blithe said. She turned to the other woman in the back of the wagon. 'Nycie, let the girl go! She needs to breath.'

Blithe shoved Kat's mother off the girl, but she kept trying to hold her daughter.

'My baby. What have they done to my baby,'

'The blade's poisoned,' Blithe said.

'W-what does that mean?'

'She's dying,'

Nyclementia and Anya both sobbed loudly.

Blithe allowed the women to wail. She never understood why it was women found the need to wail. It never solved anything. She looked out into the dark fields through which they raced. The horses breathing was laboured. They wouldn't be able to keep this up, and she doubted Kat would make the night, but she was fighter. She had to make it. Her thoughts cast out into the night, and she took a deep breath. *Talon, where are you my son?*

Talon jerked awake, sweating. The dense branches of the trees above him trapped the sun's heat leaving Talon to slow cook in the natural oven. His blanket lay next to him. He must have thrown it off sometime during the morning. He rose from his sleeping mat and shed several layers of clothing. A few paces away, he thrashed in the cool water of the stream, taking large gulps or throwing handfuls down his back.

'Thayer?' he said, looking up refreshed. The horse was not in his makeshift bed.

Talon sprinted up the hill back toward the path. It was further away from their camp than he would have guessed. He fell out of the brush in to the dirt road, and search up and down it both ways.

'Thayer!' he yelled. His voice echoed back at him giving him a start.

He listened intently, but could hear nothing, other than the sound of water below, or the rustling of leaves in the warm breeze. The horse was gone. Panic set in. He returned to the calm stream stumbling several times in his haste. *Would he have returned to the village? I can't go back now. M'ma would never let me leave. If I got back she would... lock me up and the women....*

Talon immediately regretted not taking one of the Tinsden horses. They were known for miles as the most reliable creatures for any journey. It was the reason their business did so well, or had done so well. Who knew what would happen with them now.

'Arrrgh!' he screamed.

His angry voice shouted back at him through the trees. Spinning frantically on his heels, allowing the rage and frustration to burrow through him, Talon kicked at the dirt and the leaves on the ground sending dust everywhere – over his blanket, his pillow and all over his travel sack.

I have to continue on foot and probably buy a horse in Weston. Although, if Thayer had some sense he might have continued on toward the the Gerrund farm, about half a day's ride from here I think.

Wild horses were known to roam those fields because of their famous grazing grounds. So many travellers used to stop over at the Gerrund farm on their journeys that the old couple built an inn to cater for them.

What's the time?

Talon looked up instinctively to see how far the sun had risen, but could not tell through the shade of the forest. The sunlight cast tiny dots of light over his beige shirt and brown trousers. The forest smelled like wet grass, but there had not been rain for some time. Perhaps it was the dew.

If I jogged the rest of the way I could make it there by night. They know M'ma well. I could ask to loan a horse, if they haven't seen Thayer.

Mister Gerrund's sons would be working the fields and would certainly spot a white stallion trotting by like it owned the kingdom. Talon was sure the horse had sustained monumental damage to its brain in its final battle. Thayer had survived that battle, his father had not. He pulled out his water skins from his travel sack and filled these to the brim. Then he packed up and ran back to the road.

The first thing he did was search the skies for the sun to determine how late in the day it was. It was early afternoon. He had slept half the day away. The horse had half a day on him if indeed it continued, but if it returned it would be traipsing back into the village by now.

What would M'ma do? Come after me? Send others? Talon needed to move. Before he set off he turned back, taking a moment to search for something familiar on the path that would returned him to his village. A large part of him wanted to return, but the visions of that last look Kat gave him haunted him.

COWARD. The voices of the village women echoed in his head.

Reluctantly, afraid and wholly nervous, he turned around and began on the road towards the Gerrund farm, aware of how much catching up he needed to make.

The sweltering heat of the sun's rays tampered with Talon's plan to jog most of the way. After several kilometres he abandoned the plan, instead walking at as reasonable a pace as could be expected in the heat carrying such a heavy burden. His travel sack contained all he would need for a lengthy journey.

The air felt thick and sticky; his lungs struggled to process it. His clothes were completely dry on the outside, but his sweat kept the insides moist. He half jogged for a short distance then slogged on for a longer distance, before he attempted a half-jog again. This was the remainder of his day. Meanwhile, the sun crept along the sky towards the horizon, casting an orange glow over the green landscape as it sunk.

The only thoughts that propelled him forward now were those of a violent nature in which he imagined thousands of ways of killing his father's flippant horse. His favourite so far was spending some of his hard-earned coin to purchase an axe just so that he could sink it into the horse's neck. That would teach it to abandon him.

What would father say of his fine steed now abandoning his only child to the elements and at the start of the journey no less? He spat angrily and continued in this fashion, glad for a rare cool breeze when it came along. He was even happier when the forest finally ended and opened into long rolling grass fields that stretched on for kilometres into the horizon as far as his eye could see. The crimson sun disappeared behind the hills, giving way to a moonless night littered with stars of every kind. The air was still humid, but at least it was tolerable. Summer was fast approaching if not already upon them.

A few hours in the dark, and Talon felt the gradual decline in the hills. He climbed the last hill overlooking the valley in which the Gerrund farm was located. It had been years since he and his M'ma had visited the family. It would be good to see them again. He once had the biggest crush on Emily, their daughter of similar age to him. This was before he met Kat.

It was only when Talon drew closer that he discerned something was awry with the farm. He jogged the last kilometre towards the building, until the blur of lights he saw made sense. The main building was a smouldering black heap, standing only because it had been built out of hard stone.

The entire crop fields were brutishly harvested, the remnants set ablaze. Talon felt the warmth of the ash lingering. It all smelled of burnt grass. The closer he got the more poignant the stench grew. He approached the rubble cautiously. His ears scanned every sound suspiciously from the swooshing of unburnt grass stalks to the soft sigh of the evening winds.

The silence struck Talon. Insects and animals alike seemed to have fled the scene. The forest which usually teemed with wildlife was left in a deafening silence of death and decay. *The Barbarians,* Talon thought. Somehow, in the wake of him losing Thayer, he forgot that there were ruthless beasts that would kill and destroy a farm like this without pause. They would have had no warning.

The Barbarians left only a vast chasm of destruction in their wake. The Gerrund family were a kind bunch always willing to help travellers along their journeys. They were his hope for shelter for that evening, but there was no sign of them anywhere. Talon searched the surrounding fields and called after them, there were no signs of any bodies either, just the remains of a once peaceful farm in the languid grass lands left in ruin.

Talon ventured off to the nearby treeline. He set up a tiny camp just within the shadows of this treeline, so that he could look out onto the farm house as well as in both directions on which the road travelled along. For a long while he lay there and watched the remains of the farm smoulder. It was well in to the night, too late to hunt, too late to make a run for water and too dark. He took out a small portion of bread and filled it with some cheese. He ate this and drank water. He would have preferred a pot of tea, but knew it would not be wise. After his meal, he closed his eyes.

He jumped up and reach in to his travel sack. His father's sword. It was not there. It was on Thayer's side. He was defenceless. He picked up the larges stick he could and shaking, waited for a Barbarian to appear out of the veils of darkness. The sky was growing lighter. A few moments passed by revealing that it was all in his head. He dropped the stick, and looked back to the ruins of the farm. The scene looked even worse now that there was some light. On the Eastern horizon, the sky glowed blue.

Was this what I should expect wherever I go? Ruined buildings and ruined lives? Where is the Royal Army? How could they allow so many Barbarians to roam free in our lands destroying everything in their path?

Talon couldn't sleep. He was too filled with fear, too alert. He decided to continue on his journey in the cool night air. He found himself enjoying the walk under the stars. The wind in the grass hills serenaded him as he walked on, putting him in a dreamlike daze so that when he finally looked back he could not identify the farm house in the distance at all. Weston, the next village was a full day's ride along the dusty road, which was already the width of two carriages indicating to him that he was making progress on his journey. To keep himself entertained and to distract himself from his building hunger, Talon cast his thoughts towards what he would be doing today if Prince Calren had never come to the village, and the Barbarians never attacked it.

He wrestled with himself for a long time before settling on the events of a day he thought made sense. He would have woken up that morning and gone off to do his chores as usual. He would have done them noisily and clumsily, and fought with Thayer as he did so. The creature seemed to take the greatest pleasure in pestering him. He was sure if a horse could laugh that the darned creature would laugh every morning as it kicked the trough or distracted him with his incessant snorting and grunting. He would be glad of being done with his chores and would return to the house to a great smelling kitchen full of M'ma's wonderful cooking. The aroma of freshly baked bread would waft about luring him in, but he would be scolded as usual for trying to eat without washing up. He would on occasion steal an item of food to sustain him while he got ready. Sometimes he would get caught and receive a wallop, but not on his fictional day. This day he would get away with it and sink his teeth longingly into a crunchy toasted loaf of sugar bread. His current stomach grumbled jealously at his hypothetical stomach's great fortune.

He would return to the kitchen after washing up, would have two servings of everything. He usually ate more than two people combined because M'ma usually cooked for as many. The servings would fulfil his immense appetite, which apparently, he inherited from his mother. His stomach protested so Talon skipped over the details of breakfast in his mind. Rather, he imagined himself greeting his M'ma and running off to one of the Masters for his lessons. He would begrudgingly meet the other boys of his age outside the respective Master's house to learn the craft from that Master. All the lessons of the village were practical ones. There were Masters in the world and each Master took on one or two apprentices that helped him or her develop his or her craft and in return the apprentices would earn their own skills in the craft until they too became Masters.

In his imaginary day, he pictured himself before the large workshop of Master Kamis, the village carpenter. He was a kind man with balding grey hair and a fiercely long and untamed beard. He would allow the boys to huddle together around his workshop and show them how to use the rig he developed himself. It was a large device that sawed wood faster and more accurately than those done by hand. He had developed this himself. Master Kamis would smile a toothy grin and ask for volunteers, selecting any boy. Talon was never picked, but today in his dream world he was chosen. He held the board steady and edged it forward ever so slightly to allow Master Kamis to cut the wood precisely. The other boys applauded the way they usually did for the volunteer.

Talon ran through the scenarios in which he and the other boys would be broken up into teams to conduct various tasks together, all at varying stages of the carpentry process. The outcome would be pristinely cut, and varnished planks that could be delivered in bundles of ten to the builders of the village for the various construction projects they were commission for. It felt good having purpose, he himself was never good at any of the tasks required in the village and hence he was recommended to go and train with the other boys in his case, although those boys were usually absurdly tall, or strong, features keenly sought after by the Royal Army. He was tall but of average build and so again it was only with reluctance that the old soldiers accepted him to train with them, hoping that they could mould him into something. Even in his own dream world he could envisage the scary faces of the soldier Masters glaring angrily at him fail at every task put before him. *You're too slow Talon. You're too weak Talon. You're too daft Talon.*

He shivered at the thought and took note of his surroundings. The hills were decreasing in frequency allowing him to see further into the horizon. The grass grew shorter as he travelled along and the faint glow of pre-morning glimmered on the eastern horizon's edge. The sun rose and he continued on the road to Weston with his heavy travel sack on his shoulders. Since the Gerrund farm, there were no signs of a large barbarian force moving through the country. This both worried Talon and gave him a sense of relief. He was not too sure what he would do if he ran in to them without a horse and in broad day light.

Returning to his dream world, he pictured doing what he had always done every afternoon since he was seven. He pictured himself running through the dense brush along his usual path toward the cotton field after all the day's lessons and chores were complete. The first thing he would notice was Kat's golden locks gliding in and among the sea of cotton balls. She loved to swirl around in them and send puffs of cotton in to the air around her. She would hum a tune while she did this. She always told him she imagined she was at some large fancy ball. It was a sight he could never get tired off. Some days he would rush in immediately and greet her, and on other occasions he would watch her for a song or two and allow his heart to fill with love and admiration.

In his fictional day, he waited a moment watching her dance and hum in the spray of cotton showers. He would call to her and she would start every time and turn to face him beaming and waving as he raced over to her. They would hug and fall into the field speaking over each other excitedly to tell each other about their respective days. He would tell her about being teased again and she would listen staring deeply into his eyes. He was sure he blushed every time she did that. He would listen as she explained how her chores and lessons were a success and how everyone praised her, but how much she wanted to fight for the Royal Army and how all the women mocked her for her views.

Kat would go on one of her famous rants about how women could do anything men could. He would encourage her as she did. She would mock fight cotton ball soldiers and monsters with a stray stick-sword and demonstrate to him just how fierce a woman could be in battle. He would laugh at her commentary about men's stupidity and their pompous natures. And she would give up her battle and crumple into a laughing heap next to him and get serious. They would discuss their dreams and their futures and what it is that they wanted to do. She would explain to him how she wanted to join the army to show the men that a woman could, and then she would climb the ranks and then implement changes that would revolutionise the military so that they could put an end to the Barbarian Wars once and for all.

Then she would tell of how she would turn her attention to politics and help the helpless long forgotten by the king in his depression. Talon imagined the hours they would spend talking and laughing and mock fighting in the field as the sun set. They would head off home, he would walk her to hers and occasionally join the Darringers for dinner at the insistence of Mrs Darringer and the utter horror of Mr Darringer, who would find any reason to mock Talon. Kat would defend him against her father who would leave with a red face shooed off by Mrs Darringer. She always gave Mr Darringer a menacing look for the way he treated Talon. They would enjoy dessert and tea and talk the hours away. He loved the way Kat spoke freely with her mother, sometimes he would just listen quietly as they did. And after this pleasant day, Kat would kiss him goodbye on his cheek. It was the highlight of every day, and he would walk home with a smile and fall asleep looking forward to that very same moment the next day.

'Hiho,' someone said.

Talon was ripped out of his reverie and looked up to see who had greeted him. A young man, not too much older than him, stood in front of him drawing a cart with one donkey. Both donkey and man chewed on a stalk of straw.

'Ey what's ye matter?' he said.

'What?' Talon asked.

'Ye be tearing pally,' he said.

Talon touched his hand to his cheeks and became aware of the streak of tears under each eye. He swiped at these. The donkey eh-awed at him.

'None me business of course,' he said. 'Where ye headed?'

'Have you seen my horse?' Talon asked.

The young man whistled. 'People from where ye come from not know how te greet proper?'

'What?' Talon asked.

'Said ye call that a greeting pally?'

'Oh, sorry, I am just – I'm looking for my horse,' Talon said. 'A giant white stallion.'

'White stallion ey? 'Look'd like a knight's horse and what not? Whew,' the man whistled. 'That there be one crazy horse pally, I tell ye. I seen people try te bring it in o'er near Weston and boy did they get a kicking.'

Talon clicked his tongue angrily. 'That stupid horse!'

'Stupid horse?'

'Yes, it's lost its wits a long time ago,'

'Well can't blame a witless horse if the owner go take it out fer a spin,'

Talon blinked awkwardly at the statement.

'Say ye be hungry?' the young man said.

As if in response, Talon's stomach growled loudly.

'Ye look like ye about ready to enter the afterlife,' the man observed taking off his straw hat and squinting at Talon. 'There be a tree up ahead, what say we break bread o'er there and ye can tell me ye woes?'

Talon nodded.

'Name's Jon,' The young man said.

'Talon,' he replied.

Jon pulled the cart over to the side, pulled some straw out from a bag, and held out a handful for his donkey. The animal ate it all up. They climbed back in to the cart and headed back the way Talon had come, to a set of nearby trees. They sat on the grass under the shade and ate the sandwiches that Jon produced from a brown bag as Talon recapped his story to Jon thus far. Talon gobbled up all of his sandwiches, so Jon offered up his own as well. Talon thanked him and squashed the entire thing into his mouth, chewing several times, then swallowing the thing whole, almost choking.

'Easy there pally,' Jon said slapping Talon on the back. 'No need te rush the meal or te rush te yer grave.'

He passed Talon a flask. Talon nodded and took a large swig of the warm liquid. He spat some of it out on to the grass.

'First time drinkin' Faers?' Jon chuckled.

Talon nodded.

'Usually a father's duty te give his boy his first Faers,'

'He's dead,' Talon said, taking another swig. 'My father... I mean.'

'Whew,' Jon said. 'Ye the unluckiest summabich I e'er came 'cross aren't ye?'

Talon took a final swig of the liquid that made his insides tingle. He handed the flask back.

'Well been me pleasure introducin' ye te yer first Faers – cheers!' He took a big gulp and put the flask away to Talon's dismay.

'Thank you for lunch Jon,' Talon said.

'No problem at all,' Jon said. 'And I tell ye what. I got sympathy fer ye plight, and will take you back some the ways te save ye some time. What ye say te that?'

'Ah thank you, thank you so much,' Talon said shaking the young man's hand.

'Right you are pally. Hop on te me fancy express, and let's get ye te Weston ey?'

Talon nodded and climbed up on to the cart after Jon. A moment later they were headed on the road to Weston, refreshed after their meal and their drink.

'Say, why ye goin' te Weston an'ways?' Jon asked.

To kill someone. Talon thought.

'Nowhere else to go,' he said. They rode on in silence.

'Oy pally,' Jon whispered. 'We be here.'

Talon groaned and dug further under his coat. A sliver of drool hung out the corner of his mouth.

'What business?' said a deep grumbling voice from somewhere in front of them.

'Just deliverin' young Mr Telmache ere,'

'Telmache ey?' the deep voice said. 'What business he have ere?'

'Same as any,' Jon said.

'Oh, I doubt that,' the man said. 'Lot a dubious characters comin' an' goin' these days.'

'Young Telmache ere ain't one of 'em, I can tell ye that,'

There was silence. Then the cart lurched forward. The movement jolted Talon awake.

'What's happening?' Talon asked.

'We be ere,' Jon said.

Talon blinked fatigue out of his eyes and stretched. 'Here?'

'Weston, pally,' Jon said.

Talon looked around. Thick stone brick buildings rose on either side of the cobbled road. Every few feet a street lamp protruded from the stone pavement. Each lamp stood taller than even the tallest man.

They approached the top of the road where two young boys worked together to light the candles behind the glass of each lamp. One boy manoeuvred a trolley with a large protruding ladder attached to its top. The other boy swayed ominously at the top of the ladder. His twig of an arm held a lit torch to the nearest candle which burst in to flames. He closed the lamp cover over the flame, and there was light.

'Isn't he afraid,' Talon asked. They passed the two boys by.

'Them lads?' Jon asked. 'What they got ter be 'fraid fer?'

'Falling, hurting themselves,' Talon said.

'No use being 'fraid,' the young man said.

They entered a large square with a circular fountain in the centre. Some creature Talon did not recognise stood atop the centrepiece and sprouted water from its mouth which fed the trough. Everything in the town was cast in large black-brown bricks, from the cobbled roads, to the large houses and shops which sprouted like wild mushrooms in all directions.

End of our journey together pally,' Jon said, pulling back on the reigns. 'If I were ye, I would check with James Flatry, the Weston stable master. If there been a horse traipsing 'bout he be sure to know,'

'Thank you Jon,' Talon said.

'Not a thing,'

'Okay then,' Talon said grabbing his large rucksack.

'Oh!' Jon exclaimed. 'Since ye seem ter like yer Faers so much, I recommends ye stop by the Ol' Weston. They have the best Faers, if ye can stand the Barbarians.'

'Barbarians?' Talon said. 'Here in Weston.'

'That's right,' Jon said. 'We be overrun I tell ye, but they seem ter mind their own business least.'

'Did you see them come in? Did they have a prisoner with them?'

'Prisoner?' Jon said scratching his head under his straw hat. 'I ain't seen no prisoner. What's all this 'bout?'

'Nothing, thank you for the safe passage,' Talon said. He jumped off the cart and nodded at Jon.

'Best a luck pally,' Jon said waving his hat and ushering his donkey onwards.

Talon skipped across the square past carriages clattering loudly in all directions. There were four directions he could go down. He intercepted a burly woman wearing a black and purple corset which did well to hide her girth and accentuate her cleavage.

'Peace to you miss,' Talon greeted.

'Peace to me indeed young sir,' she said. 'What will it be?'

'What?' Talon asked frowning.

The woman grabbed him by the small of his back and drew him close so that his cheeks pressed against her bosom. 'Don't toy now, that ain't polite.'

'Can – Ca-,' Talon tried to speak in to her breasts, while struggling to free himself. He pried himself loose of her grip, stumbled a few feet away and made sure to keep a safe distance from her probing tentacles. 'The Old Weston. Do you know where it is?'

'The Ol' Weston?' The woman sang. 'Oh well I found the last gentleman in all of the kingdom.'

'You what?'

'Willing to dine a woman before he had his way with her,' she declared. Passers-by stared at the two of them.

Talon panicked and ran in the opposite direction as fast as he could. He crashed into something large.

'Move!' the moving mass grunted.

Talon looked up. A bear of a man glared down at him. He grimaced at Talon who fell to the floor and cowered in to a corner. The rest of the crowd kept a safe distance from the scene, but the barbarian turned around and continued on his way. The crowd stopped holding its breath and all the town folk continued about their business.

Talon sat on the ground waiting for his heartbeat to restore itself, but it continued to pound away loudly against his chest. Slowly, he picked himself off the floor. *Follow him.* A wild thought. He looked in the direction the Barbarian disappeared in.

A gust of wind swept past Talon. He paused. Then, he moved. He squeezed through the crowded streets, searching up and down. A waft of tangy perfumes, spices, and cooked meat hit him. He paid no attention to the direction he was headed in the maze of new and unfamiliar streets. Finally, to his left, he saw the large towering bulk of the barbarian disappear around a corner at the top of the road. Talon pursued, apologising to those he bumped past violently.

He turned the corner but the barbarian was no longer there. Talon walked along the road moving with the crowd, while searching both left and right in the adjacent alleys or roads. *Where is he?*

A short way along, he found a street vendor scrambling to pick up his ham slices off the ground. The crowd ignored the man as he frantically scooped up his wares. Talon, stopped to help. The man grabbed Talon's hand as he picked up one of the slices.

'I'm helping,' Talon said. He placed the ham slice he had back on the vendor's broken stand. The vendor thanking him through a mumbled breath, and they continued picking up the assorted meats cast on the floor.

Once they were done Talon enquired after what had happened. 'Was it the barbarian? Did he come this way?'

The man nodded and scurried off with his broken cart.

'Which way did he go?' Talon called after the man.

Without a word, the vendor looked up the road and then scrambled down the nearest alley. Talon continued his pursuit. At the top of the road, an audible commotion rang from the right. The entire street was packed with barbarians, most of them swaying and grunting to some or other tune, but each had in his hand a large jug of golden liquid. *Faers.*

Talon edged towards the source of the commotion. *Why are the barbarians not attacking the town?* A gust of wind swept past him kicking dust in to the air. The skies rumbled almost angrily. Talon looked up, it was night but he couldn't see the moon or starts. A storm was coming. The barbarians were too drunk to notice him. He must have been inconsequential to them, too small, too weak to pose a threat, and so he walked amongst them stopping in front of a large double storey building with large windows on either side of the door. It was a public house, with many diverse people inside, dancing, and singing and drinking. Ecstatic music blared from inside, concealed by the crowd of people dancing enthusiastically. The bass of the drums vibrated in his chest. The crowd began to clap loudly in synchronisation to the music. Above the brown oak door stood an ancient, dilapidated sign written in gold which read: *Th Old We ton.*

This was the place Jon had told him about. The crowd parted momentarily. Time slowed. His eyes widened. Every fibre of his being tensed. On the other side of the glass sat the man he wanted to kill. *Drag'a.* The crowd shifted again and his target disappeared.

The ground rushed towards him. He stumbled to his right and found himself leaning against a grubby wall. He threw up. His hands shook so he clenched them into a fists.. His insides squirmed. Talon coughed to clear his throat and spat to clear his mouth of the metallic taste. He hit the wall.

A loud thud echoed near him, giving him a fright. He jumped against the wall at the entrance of the alleyway where he stood. Shadows danced violently against the walls around the corner. Loud guttural moans were exchanged and then more thunderous thuds.

A vibrating crack made the hair on Talon's arm stand on end. There was a fierce roar in response and then the clanging of weapons. Talon looked back at the road. The barbarians were unaware of the scuffle. Half-dressed women and other strays mingled amongst them. The giants weren't that frightening without their animal masks. The rhythmic thud, thud, thud, of the drums inside reverberated through the wall and his palm. The crowd cheered.

He crept against the wall as though his life depended on it. At the end of the alley, he knelt and poked his eye around the corner in time to see a large sword thrust through the bulk of a gigantic barbarian warrior, draped in the customary black.

The wielder of the blade, slowly drove it deeper so that every inch crept through the wounded barbarian's back. The large barbarian fell to the floor, coughing blood as he did. The victor, another barbarian warrior, came into sight once the barbarian fell away. He had an axe securely lodged in the side of his skull, almost comically. He too was draped in the warrior black. He saw Talon and roared. Talon recoiled but the barbarian fell forward with such force, the axe broke free taking a piece of his skull with him.

Talon's eyes widened, and his pulse throbbed painfully in his throat. He turned to run and to never stop running.

'Talon?' a voice whispered.

6

The Ol' Weston

Talon's heart sank as he turned around slowly. In all the commotion, he failed to see the cage on top of a wooden wagon on the far side of the cobbled courtyard at the end of the alleyway.

'Oh, thank the king! Talon!' a shadowy figure coughed. He grabbed the bars.

Talon crept closer avoiding the bloody remnants of the barbarian warriors. Talon gagged when he stepped on a bloody finger. He jumped over the bodies and made his way to the cage, squinting through the dark.

'Prince Calren?'

'Talon! It is you. I wasn't dreaming. Thank the king,' he said. 'Who are you here with?'

Talon frowned. The lamp from the adjacent street cast an eerie orange glow on to the walls of the alley.

'Where's Kat? Is she safe?' he asked.

'Kat?' Talon said dazed.

'Yes,'

Talon swallowed the lump in his throat and fought away tears.

'Spit it out!'

'She's…' Talon began softly. His voice broke. He couldn't say it.

He looked at the prince. His face was swollen to twice its size on the right-hand side. His nose sat at an odd angle with a trail of dried blood leading out of each nostril. One of his eyes was completely shut, and a dark purple. He could barely squint out of the other. He still wore his wedding clothes, richly embroidered golden robes. This was ripped, in various places, covered in dirt and blood.

'Talon,' he shouted.

'She's...' he repeated. He choked and began crying. He shook his head.

'No!' the prince said. He sunk to a limp heap on the cage floor.

'Where are the others?' Prince Calren asked. 'There has to be others. They'll tell you you're wrong.'

'There's no one else here,' Talon said. 'All the men are dead. Some women and children too.'

The prince was dead silent for a moment. He didn't move, didn't breathe. 'W-why are you here? How?'

'I was...' he began.

'Running away?' the prince finished.

'No,' Talon said. He cast his head down avoiding Prince Calren's eyes. 'Yes.'

'WHY?' he roared. 'Kat's dead and you, you...'

'I didn't have a choice,' he said.

'We always have a choice man!' he shouted. 'How could you?'

'Keep you voice down,'

'MY VOICE? ARE YOU MAD? YOU COWARD! DON'T YOU DARE...'

'I w-was afraid okay?'

'We all are you fool!' The prince said. 'None of that matters... if she's... no she can't be. I won't believe it.'

'I saw it,'

'AND DID NOTHING!'

Talon cringed. He was crying.

'YOU DON'T GET TO CRY FOR HER!'

Talon shook his head and shrugged his shoulders.

'Just leave,' Prince Calren said defeated. 'Leave me alone. Run away like the coward you are.'

'I'm...' Talon said.

Prince Calren turned around into a ball.

'I'm going to kill him,' Talon said.

Nothing.

'For what he did,' Talon explained. 'I promise.'

The prince chuckled. 'What does the promise of a coward mean to me? How are you going to do what no one in the history of the kingdom has managed to do?'

'I don't care,' Talon said. 'I will. For Kat.'

'It's like you never even knew her, not really,' the prince said. 'Leave. Or I'll shout.'

Talon stayed there.

'HELP! THERE IS AN INTRUDER!' the prince screamed at the top of his lungs.

Talon backed away into the shadows and then returned to the front of the building ending up lost in thought standing before the large oak door. A profound sense of dread welled up inside of him, threatening to drown him. A powerful force shoved him forward through the ancient wooden door. He spilled across the dirty tavern floor. After a moment, he sneezed lifting a cloud of dirt and sending the dust in all directions. The floorboards moaned under the bump and thud of dancing feet around him.

A large shadow draped in black disappeared into the swinging and swaying crowd chuckling. Boisterous music blared from the other side of the large room. A barbarian, possessed by the music, beat loudly on a set of yellowing animal drums. A lanky fellow with shoulder long hair plucked away at a circular stringed instrument.

A thick arm crept under his shoulder and hoisted him up effortlessly. He stood before a sturdy man with a long, thick black beard, almost a head shorter than Talon, at least double his age, and covered in soot.

'Right ther' laddie?' The man asked jovially.

Talon nodded, and scanned the buzzing room.

'First time, ey?' the man beamed through his beard.

Talon smiled nervously.

The man signalled Talon to follow him and slipped around a pair of young maidens dripping in sweat. He took a moment to appreciate the way their bodies gyrated to the crazy music, then followed the sturdy man.

They arrived at a long table in the back, near the stage where the mismatched musicians played their strange instruments. There were more dirty men seated around the table, each with a jug filled with golden elixir. His rescuer arrived at the table first. He received tumultuous roars from his peers. He pointed to Talon and shouted something. They cheered and pulled up a chair for him.

He shook each of their grubby hands as they were introduced, 'Rood, Barlin, Grinner, Ven, and I be Hammon,'

'Talon,'

'Louder laddie,' Hammon shouted.

'TALON,' he said pointing to himself.

'TALON!' the men cheered, lifting their large jugs.

As Talon sat down Hammon, seated on his left, reached past him and grabbed the hand of petite young women. She wore a short sky-blue dress that barely covered her bare bronze legs.

Hammon whispered something in her ear. She grinned and glanced at Talon. His heart skipped a beat. The mad drumming of the quick music reverberated in his chest. Talon looked away for a moment. A short, fiercely-freckled women with orange curls muttered incantations into a long horn that sent her voice bouncing off the walls of the tavern.

'Hiya,'

Talon turned around in time to see the young woman sink in to his lap. Gracefully, she flung a thin bronze arm around his neck, so that her exposed cleavage pressed against his face.

'H-h -,' Talon mumbled. He cleared his throat. 'Hiya,'

'I be Sameen,' she whispered in his ear. Her scent floated gently off of her neck. It smelled like freshly budded roses after the first rains.

'Talon,' he blurted.

Sameen giggled. 'Yer friends tell me this is yer firs' time,'

'First time?' he glanced at them with surprise. They raised their jugs with pride.

'In a tavern, silly boy,'

'Oh, yeah,' he chuckled anxiously.

'How can I be of service?'

Talon gulped, and looked to the men for help. They laughed.

'A big, fresh jug of yer best Faers for me young friend miss,' Hammon shouted. He winked at Talon.

'Coming up,' Sameen said. She turned back to Talon and kissed him on the cheek. 'Save my seat?'

He nodded wide-eyed and she disappeared into the crowd of people.

'AYYYY TALON!' the men cheered. 'Welcome te the Ol' Weston ey!'

Talon was relieved to have a moment to catch his breathe. Once again the music changed, and the crowd clapped along to the beat and stamped their feet in unison, adding to the hypnotic effect.

Coins talk here Master Talon,' Hammon said smiling. 'Else them beauties pay you no mind.'

He pointed over at the next table where a portly man in fine clothes slipped a large gold coin in between the cleavage of a pale maiden with long golden curls. Talon had to remind himself to close his mouth.

'Ay, but 'tis alright te feel loved if you can spare the loot,' Rood shouted from the end of the table. The miners chuckled to themselves.

A veil of scented smoke wafted lazily through the room. Some clouds had different colours, like sky blue or orange and purple. Barlin pulled a pipe from inside his grey cloak and began stuffing it with green tobacco which smelled like apples.

'Best te be careful of them wenches,' Ven scowled. 'They'll do anything for a coin. Convince ye they love ye, all fire and passion 'til ye last silver piece!'

'Ye just bitter ye spent ye whole wage in one night!' Grinner said.

The miners roared with laughter. Ven frowned and shook his head. Barlin lit his pipe and puffed away. Thick lime clouds streamed out of his nostrils and mouth. The sweet smells of fresh fruit and flowers wafted above their table and mixed with the scent of food and the tang of the perfumes and sweat from the room. The entire scene was hypnotic. The room was dimly lit, with only a few lanterns burning along the wooden walls. Large wooden beams stretched across the ceiling from one end to the other, and above that lay thick black thatch roofing.

'So what brings ye te these parts Master Talon?' Ven asked still scowling. He sat on Talon's right clutching his half empty jug. He was the youngest of the men, and the only one taller than Talon at the table.

'Uhm, I am…' Talon started. 'On an adventure, you could say.'

'Adventure ey?' Grinner said. He sat on Ven's right. 'Ain't a man alive not looking fer bit a that ey?'

'Here we are my love,' Sameen said. Without warning she slipped into Talon's lap, her generous dark curls falling past her shoulder. She flipped her hair to the other side so her cheek could touch his. This also gave Talon a better view of her breasts. 'I have te see ye take yer first sip. Bottom's up!'

Talon drew the heavy jug to his face nervously and took a large swig. The golden liquid was ice cold, but felt warm and tingled as it made its way down his throat. His head grew light as he drank, but he only stopped when he finished half of the drink. He slammed his jug down on the table and burped loudly. His spectators cheers unanimously, but his face turned scarlet.

Sameen hugged him close to her breasts. 'What about ye all? No Faers fer ye?'

'Coin love,' Hammon said. 'spent the last on young Master Talon here,' Hammon said.

'Lucky boy.' Sameen jumped up to leave, but Talon grabbed her hand.

'Get us another round Sameen!' Talon said loudly with a grin.

The miner's sat up.

'Woh laddie, Faers be a silver coin a piece,' Grinner said.

Talon dug into the pouch on his belt and pulled out a gold coin. Sameen's eyes lit up and Talon's new friends roared with pride!

'Ye heard the lad love, five of yer best!'

'Aren't ye full of surprises love,' Sameen said. 'Five o' the best comin' up!' She danced away into the crowd.

'Pray tell o this adventure Master Talon,' Rood said. He was very soft-spoken, but the bulkiest of the men. 'Any work for humble folk such as ourselves?'

Talon scanned their faces.

'Maybe,' Talon said.

Each man stared at him intensely waiting for him to continue. Barlin passed his pipe to Ven, who puffed away frantically in anticipation.

'A few days ago,' Talon paused to take another sip of his Faers, then sat forward. The miners did the same. 'A few days ago, my village was attacked.'

He slammed his hand on the table for affect. The men jumped in their seats and stared at each other awkwardly.

'Hiya lads,' a man said to Talon's right.

The miners jumped again.

'Beg your pardon,' he said. He wore a dark green cloak, with the hood drawn to conceal his face. 'It was not my intention to frighten you. I was just hoping I could buy some tobacco from you?'

'Ye can have the last of this,' Barlin said throwing over a tiny pouch. The man grabbed it out of the air gracefully.

'Many thanks,' he said bowing. 'Have a good evening now.'

The miners nodded and turned back to Talon.

'Who attacked yer?' Grinner asked.

'Barbarians,' he said pausing. 'They killed most of the villagers, including…'

'Includin' who?' Barlin asked.

'My best friend!'

The group fell silent.

'So what ye goin' te do?' Grinner asked.

Talon remain silent.

'Nothin' te do,' Rood said plainly.

Talon turned around in his chair and searched the room, he could not see Drag'a.

'They have Prince Calren,' Talon said. 'In the alley out back. Caged and beaten.'

The miners whistled.

'Impossible,' Hammon said. The future king is caged in the back?'

'See for yourself if you don't believe me,' Talon said taking another drink. 'He was going to marry my best friend – well technically they were married for all but a minute, before they attacked.'

'Don't think we can help with all that Master Talon,' Ven said.

'Them is a scourge in me bones, but there be not much that can be done. Them is *barbarians* after all,' Barlin whispered, looking over his shoulders to ensure he was not overheard.

'I'm going to kill their leader,' Talon said. He finished his drink.

The men cast glances between them.

'H-how ye goin' manage that Master Talon?' Grinner asked.

'He's sitting over there,' Talon pointed behind him.

Hammon whistled loudly. Barlin, Grinner and Ven gulped loudly. Rood placed his face in his hands.

'Here we go boys. Six Faers – I threw in an extra one for young Master Talon,' Sameen said. She delivered all six jugs on to the centre of the table, making a point of arching her back when she did. The men sat in silence. 'What be the matter with ye?'

'Sameen,' Talon said. 'I need your help.'

'Depends what kind love,'

'Could you go over that way, and see if there is a barbarian, fancy looking, different from the rest, lean and tall with cold eyes,'

'Yeah?'

'Could you give him a drink and find out if he has a key around his neck,'

'I don' know love,'

Talon placed a gold coin on the table. Sameen crossed her arms and shifted her weight nervously.

'Give him a drink and say it's from a friend, then check if he has a key around his neck and tell me. The rest of the money is yours,'

She looked at him for a moment and then at the gold coin. She nodded so he slid the gold coin across the table towards her. She snatched it up and disappeared into the crowd.

'Bottoms up,' Talon said. He reached for his drink. The miners did the same.

'Master Talon,' Rood piped up. 'Why not jus' rescue Prince Calren and be done with it? No need te kill anybody.'

'The key is around Drag'a's neck,'

The miners gasped at the name.

'Don' say his name willy nilly!' Barlin said. 'Quickest route te the gave it is.'

'What key?'

'The key to the cage the prince is in,' Talon explained in between large gulps of his Faers.

'Ye a mighty warrior Master Talon? Trained under them Royal Knights?' Ven asked, his speech slurred slightly. He passed the pipe to Talon. 'Ye jus' puff lightly on the end and the pipe does the rest.'

Talon accepted the pipe awkwardly. He lifted it to his mouth slowly, and carefully pulled on the end, breathing in deeply as he did. He broke out in a fit of coughs which had the miners all in stiches.

'Light puffs Master Talon,' Barlin chuckled.

Talon tried again and got it right. As he exhaled a large green cloud of smoke streamed across their table. His body tingled all over.

'I'm ... not a warrior Ven,' Talon said puffing. 'But... I've been training to be one my whole life! My father was a Royal Knight ye know. So I know what to do with a sword.'

Talon offered the pipe back to Ven, who ushered him to hand it over to Hammon. The fanatical music continued in the background raising tumultuous cheers from the crowd every now and then. Talon felt the vibrations of the drums and many dancing feet all throughout his body. Rood and Barlin swayed to the beats and a jive came on seamlessly from the previous song. Again the crowd cheered.

The room was smoke-filled and hazy and filled to capacity by Talon's measure. He looked over his shoulder to try find Drag'a in the crowd. He saw the man in the green hood sitting alone in a corner puffing away on his own pipe. Other than that, he could not see Drag'a or Sameen.

Time went on and the pipe moved through all of the miners and reached Talon once again just as he finished the last of his Faers. He gladly accepted it from Ven who glanced at him through droopy eyes. Talon scanned the faces of all the miners, and realised they all looked the same, lost in deep thought, some nodding their heads to the music with their eyes closed.

'Nothin' like a good Jug-a-Faers and a good pipe ey Master Talon?' Hammon said slapping him on the back.

Talon giggled and nodded.

'Hiya boys,' a voluptuous blonde woman said. She dropped six jugs of Faers on the table filled to the brim, so that some splotched over her patrons. 'Sameen had to take her leave, but she handed me the table se jus' lemme know if ther's anything I can help ye boys with.'

'I asked Sameen to help me with something,' Talon said. Passing the pipe on.

'Don' know nothin' 'bout that Mister,' the lady said. 'Me name be Marigold – Mari fer short.'

She winked at Talon and disappeared in to the crowd.

'What ye think that means?' Hammon asked. The others listened intently.

He shook his head and search the crowd one more time. Through a gap, Talon could make Drag'a out. He sat in the midst of two beautiful maidens, his arms around each one and he was laughing. Talon slapped the table.

'Look at him,' Talon shouted. 'Enjoying life while Kat is dead!'

'Who's Kat Master Talon?' Barlin asked.

'My best...,' He swallowed. 'My best friend.'

'Ay, my apologies,' he said.

'Apologies,' the others said raising their glasses.

Talon stood up and swayed for a moment. He lifted his jug of Faers to his mouth and drank it one go. He climbed the bench and then the table so he could tower over the crowd.

He drew a deep breath and shouted at the top of his lungs, 'DRAG'A!'

Those in the crowd closest to him stopped dancing to see what the commotion was about, but the music continued to play and Drag'a continued to laugh with the women.

'Get down form there now Mister,' Mari said appearing from the crowd to his left.

Talon looked at her and shooed her away. He swayed precariously almost falling over backwards, but straightened up in time.

'Come now laddie why don' ye come down from there ey?' Hammon said standing up.

Talon threw his jug of Faers across the room. It crashed loudly on Drag'a's table, so that the women in his arms screamed as the shards launched at their bare shoulders.

'DRAG'A!' He roared so that his face turned red.

The musicians stopped playing their music abruptly and in an instant the crowd fell silent. Not one person took so much as a loud breath.

'You rotten murdering scoundrel!' Talon screamed. 'Are you deaf too?'

'I am listening,' he said in his smooth eerie voice.

'You killed my best friend you spawn of a goat!'

'Coward?' he roared with laughter that made the hair on Talon's arms stand on end. 'The coward who ran away while I killed that wannabe princess?'

'Her name was Katrina,' Talon spat.

'She was weak and pathetic,' Drag'a said.

'I challenge you to combat!'

Again Drag'a laughed. 'Someone get this fool another Faers on my tab.'

'You sack of worms, why won't you fight me? Didn't your troll of a mother teach you how to be man?' Talon hissed. 'Fight me you coward!'

Drag'a shot up and flicked his wrist in one smooth motion. Talon felt a pinch on his right-hand side. Gravity pulled him backwards and sent him crashing violently onto the dirty floor past the miners.

He thought he heard his name uttered amongst the throng of screams. The pinch in his right shoulder became a sting. All he heard was the panicked screams, and urgent shuffling of boots on the moaning wooden floorboards.

The room spun. Talon caught glimpses of the dim lights flashing. He rolled on to his back. Laying there a moment his breathing laboured, he probed his right shoulder. A blade was dug deep into his shoulder at an awkward angle all the way to the hilt. He looked up at his bloody left hand and could not bring himself to look at his wound.

Instead, Talon tried to rip the blade out, but before his fingers closed on the hilt his head was hoisted off the ground roughly by the strands of his messy brown hair. Any movement sent waves of pain down his injured right arm. He screamed all the while he was dragged to the centre of the room.

'Please, please don't fight in here I beg you Master,' A man mumbled out of Talon's field of vision. 'I'll give you and your men all the Faers in the ….'

The man stopped abruptly then fell to the floor with a loud thud. His torso came into Talon's field of vision on the left. He bled from his throat, his plate-sized eyes searching for any hope. Panic filled the man's eyes. His hands clutched at the thin line across his throat but despite his efforts, a river of blood rushed past his fat fingers. The man convulsed twice and then went limp, paler than any person should ever be.

Talon blinked at the man who stared at him blankly. He reached out to the man but was too far away. In his confusion Talon tried hoisting himself up further with his right hand, but it remained limp at his side. Without warning, the world turned again and his head hit the floor loudly.

'What's your name you fool?' the barbarian's smooth voice asked from somewhere to his right.

Talon's vision disappeared for a moment and then returned with stars floating lazily across the ceiling. He blinked them away and searched for the barbarian.

'Not much of a fight,' he said, closer this time. Something dragged across the floor, and Drag'a came in to view dragging a wooden chair. He almost fell into the chair and once settled kicked Talon in the side gently. 'More an execution if you ask me. Perhaps that is what you intended? To die?'

Talon did not respond. He blinked up at the barbarian leader. He was handsome. That more than anything else shocked Talon. All the stories he was ever told about Barbarians noted how hideous they were – monsters was the word often used. This monster did not look like a monster.

'Let the fool live,' a man said from Talon's left. Talon twisted his neck to catch a glimpse of him but could only see the dead man lying in a pool of his own blood.

'And who are you?' Drag'a asked.

'Nobody of importance,' the man said.

'You are pretty calm for the situation, he of no importance,' Drag'a said.

'No use panicking I find,' the man replied. 'Unless of course you are trying to get yourself killed.'

Silence.

Talon's eyes filled with tears. His heart pounded heavily in his chest. It was so loud he could feel his pulse in his throat and hear it drumming desperately in his ears. The more blood he lost the dizzier he grew. His vision blurred at the edges. His eyelids felt heavy.

'Stay awake boy,' the man said.

'No use, he'll be dead soon, but such a gentle death is unworthy of him,' Drag'a said.

'Killing him would be unworthy of you,' the man said. 'Have the barbarian ways changed so much?'

Drag'a scanned the man carefully. Eventually he asked, 'what do you know of the barbarian ways?'

'Not much,' the man replied.

'Not much at all,' Drag'a chuckled. 'Perhaps … one day I will teach you Kingsman,' Drag'a whispered.

The door burst open. Ear-piercing roars filled the room.

'No, these Kingsmen are mine!' Drag'a shouted.

The room fell silent again but for the heavy breathing of the barbarian warriors waiting.

'Behold, here lies the greatest coward,' Drag'a said. He looked down at Talon. 'Shame, every barbarian looks forward to *his* fight.'

Drag'a lifted his sword above Talon's chest and let it hover there for a moment. He looked up at the man across the room, then lazily, he let the blade fall. Talon closed his eyes and braced himself filling his blurry mind with thoughts of Kat. What would it be like to see her again? Would he see her again? There was a crash. He opened his eyes to find the blade lodged into the floor board just past his chest. Drag'a ripped it out of the ground and backed away from Talon.

Drag'a issued kill orders in his native tongue. The barbarians roared in response. Their heavy boots thudded loudly across the room on the old wooden floor. It sounded like three pairs of boots. The Barbarians roared again. Above them, a peel of thunder shook the foundations of the building and for a moment muted all sound. Talon waited to hear another heavy thud on the floor.

Instead, swords clanking, scraped together, and clanked again to Talon's left. He hoisted his head with the last of his strength. Nothing. His body rebelled, and still his vision continued to darken

A sharp piercing pain cut through Talon's stomach. He made to scream like he had never screamed before, but no sound escaped his mouth. By default his body doubled over and he fell to his left.

'My gift to you,' Drag'a whispered in Talon's ear, ripping his blade free from Talon's shoulder. 'Now you know what you dear women felt.'

Talon sobbed silently, as waves and waves of pain flooded through his body. He began to shiver wildly.

'Die well kingsmen,' Drag'a announced. He barked more orders at his men.

Talon caught the first glimpses of the skirmish. Three bulky barbarian warriors clad in their war furs and masks crowded around the hidden man.

One warrior sidestepped out of the way so another could thrust his thick blade at their quarry. The slender man parried the blow with a thick wooden staff, sending the blade square into the chest of the adjacent barbarian. Without pausing, the man jabbed the end of his staff into the throat of the opposite Barbarian so that both warriors fell to the floor at the same time. The man ducked a swipe of the last barbarian warrior's axe. He swung on one knee so that his back faced the barbarian. His staff hit the barbarian on the bottom of his jaw which sent him shuffling backwards. The man's forest green robes swivelled with him as he twisted back to a resting position.

Talon's head dropped involuntarily, the world on its side. He could feel a gooey liquid rise out of his mouth. His vision was now almost completely blurred. And he slowly closed his eyes.

'Don't close your eyes,' the man said.

Talon disobeyed.

Talon's cheek stung. His eyes shot open.

'There we go!' he said. 'Stay with me you fool.'

The man hoisted Talon over his shoulder, but the boy lay limp there unable to resist.

'We need to move,' the man said.

Bells rang wildly somewhere outside, but were temporarily muted by another roll of deafening thunder. He was unable to resist the heaviness in his eyelids. Blackness swirled across his vision, until there was nothing.

7

THE SAGE

Something tugged at his consciousness. Talon awoke out of a deep sleep without opening his eyes. Instead, he laid still soaking in the soothing silence. The cacophonous chirping of crickets broke the calm. He was wrapped tightly in a warm blanket, his movement limited. Slowly, he opened his eyes. Far above him, thousands upon thousands of stars glittered brightly in the empty darkness. To his left, a fire crackled away illuminating a campsite. Dim amber light from the fire illuminated a hooded figure lounged against a fallen tree not too far from him. He tried to sit up too quickly. A sharp pain slicing through his gut stopped him. He howled and writhed and cursed using every foul word that came to mind. Only once he stopped moving did the pain ease, if only slightly, enough for him to focus.

'Don't move,' a deep voice said.

'Who are you?' Talon breathed through gritted teeth. He rolled sideways on to his elbow. With great effort, he managed to hoist himself up slightly. The world spun upside down. Talon saw the ground, then the sky. He was in the air and then he was placed against a large boulder that made for a comfortable backrest. The man backed away allowing his face to come into focus. He sat back on his hind legs and drew his hood. His cold midnight blue eyes searched Talon's. The boy leant as far back into the rock as it would allow and did all he could to wrestle the pain bubbling in his gut. Still the man hovered before him with his eyes fixed on Talon.

'I am Roan,' He said finally. 'Sage of the Cerion Valleys.'
Talon stared at him blankly. *What is a Sage?*
'And you are the coward?' Roan said.
'What?' Talon choked.
'Isn't that what Drag'a called you?' the older man asked. His eyebrow rose.
'I'm Talon!'
'Talon the Coward,' Roan repeated. 'Has a ring to it.'
'No!' He snapped. 'I am not a coward.'
'You're not?' Roan said. 'Then what are you?'
'I'm...' Talon trailed off. 'I'm a knight on a quest.'
Roan chuckled and shook his head.
'What?' Talon asked.

'You're the worst knight I ever seen,' Roan said. He burst into a rolling cough of a laugh filled with mirth. The aged skin around his eyes wrinkled.

'You must not know many knights!' Talon shouted.

'Talon the Fool,' Roan said, standing up. He made his way to a pile of wood. He picked out a log lazily, then threw it into the fire. Crimson sparks burst into the air spreading the scent of pine and juniper into the air. The first sign of gloomy grey light peaked out from behind a mountain on the distant horizon. They were camped on an outcrop on top of a high hill that hovered over an extensive plain that ran in all directions for as far as the eye could see. The only break in the grasslands was the snow-capped mountain range which reminded him of a coiled-up snake ready to strike at its prey.

Talon turned his attention back to Roan. The aging man's muscles protruded through his emerald cloak for brief moments as he moved. He was tall and *precise*. The word kept repeating in Talon's head. *And dangerous.* He kept both eyes on the man, and watched his every move. His nostrils flared at the thought of how the man had dismissed the notion of him being a knight. Everyone dismissed him.

Roan pulled a thick wooden pipe from inside his coat, strode to the fire and scooped up smouldering coals to light the contents. The older man then drew a few deep puffs. He exhaled a thick cloud of scented smoke. The aroma overwhelmed Talon's nostrils. It smelled like wet grass after a summer's rain. Talon sneezed loudly sending ripples of pain up his abdomen and Roan continued to lounge against the fallen tree truck. After a few deep puffs, he looked at Talon and then back into the depths of the now roaring fire.

'Why were you in the Old Weston?' Roan asked sending a jet of smoke out the side of his mouth.

'What happened?' Talon asked.

'You got stabbed,' Roan coughed. 'Obviously.'

Talon sneezed again. 'What is that?'

'Tabac?' Roan asked holding up the pipe. 'It's flavoured tobacco, herbs and spices. Different flavours create different experiences and sensations. Want some?'

'No,' Talon coughed.

'Too bad,' Roan mumbled. 'It will calm your nerves.' A moment of silence fell over the camp allowing them to hear the wind ruffling through the leaves of a nearby tree. 'What were you doing there?'

'None of your business,'

'Might be my business,' Roan puffed. 'Seeing as I saved your life.'

'I don't even know who you are,' Talon began.

'You hard of hearing boy?' Roan asked.

'Roan, Sage of the Cerion Valleys,' Talon said.

'Perhaps you just simple then,'

'What's a sage?'

'Definitely simple,' Roan exhaled another large cloud of green smoke. 'What's a sage he says.'

'Well?'

'A sage? I am a sage. A sage is…' Roan mumbled. He sat up. 'A sage is a protector.'

'Of what?'

'Knowledge,'

'Like a keeper of books?'

Roan coughed. 'A what? How dare you?'

'Knowledge, boy knowledge, not books. Books are a means to convey knowledge, I protect the source of knowledge, not the medium,' the older man huffed.

'I don't understand,' Talon said.

'We already established that,'

Talon clicked his tongue and made to cross his arms, but the movement made him double over in agony.

'I wouldn't move if I were you,' Roan said.

'The barbarians!' Talon shouted.

'Relax,' Roan said.

'Where are we?'

'Safe,'

Talon looked around.

'Their leader…' Talon began. 'he stabbed me!'

Talon clutched his gut underneath the blankets. He felt a dressing wrapped tightly around his bare torso.

'Yes, I said that already,' Roan shook his head.

'Where are they now?'

'Long gone,'

'What do you mean?'

'I mean It's been three weeks and barbarians are deceptively fast,'

'THREE WEEKS?' Talon erupted. He howled because of his movement.

'Stop moving!' Roan said.

'I have to go!'

'You're not going anywhere anytime soon,' Roan snorted.

Talon tried to move one more time and roared with pain. A sweat broke out across his brow and his skin seared. Stars danced across his vision, he fell to his left and then vomited.

'You don't understand,' Talon mumbled lifting himself off the dirt. His belly burned. Roan swept across the outcrop and set Talon upright against the rock again. 'The prince!' Talon yelled. 'They have the prince!'

'Which prince?' Roan asked.

'Do you know of another prince?'

'Calren?' Roan puffed.

'You don't believe me, but I'm telling the truth,'

'Can't trust a coward or a fool,'

'T-they killed everyone! And they took him. I-I thought I could...'

'Could what?' Roan chuckled.

The sage moved away to the fire and continued muttering under his breath. 'What were you doing at the Old Weston?'

'He killed -' Talon breathed. 'Someone important to me.'

'Not the first time and not the last,'

'He killed Princess Katrina,' Talon hissed. The words stung worse than his belly.

'I don't know a Princess Katrina,'

'She's my – she was my...'

'Women,' Roan finished. 'How common.'

'She was Prince Calren's bride' Talon spat. 'You know what that makes her right? Or do I need to explain how royal marriage works?'

'I mighta heard about a royal marriage in some remote back-end village,'

'I –,' Talon began. 'That's where I'm from. It's Hexon Falls. It's not a back-end village.'

'Why would a renowned barbarian warlord murder a simple village maid?' Roan said.

'She wasn't a simple village maid!'

'She was in love with you, wasn't she? Had to be simple. King rest her soul!'

Talon blinked at Roan. He burst out in laughter.

'She didn't did she?' Roan chuckled. 'She didn't love you. King bless your heart boy. Yours is a pathetic story if I ever heard one.'

'Drag'a attacked Hexon Falls. That's where Prince Calren was gonna marry my, marry Kat, but the wedding was attacked. They killed all the men. The w-women kicked me out of the village, but that doesn't matter. I promised Calren I would kill Drag'a and I am going to keep that promise.'

'Great work ye making of it ey?' Roan said with a raised eyebrow. He lounged back against the log.

'Tell me ye long sap story boy while I smoke my tabac,' Roan said.

'We don't have time!'

The first rays of sunlight burst across the sky.

'Ye ain't goin' nowhere without my help and I am not helping until I know the story,'

Thayer appeared neighing. The horse was saddled with all Talon's things!

'My horse!' Talon said.

'Your horse?' Roan coughed with laughter. 'This is a knight's horse boy, a famous one.'

'Thayer, you fool horse!' Talon shouted. The horse snorted.

'You know this boy?' Roan asked the horse. Thayer whinnied and trotted off to the edge of the campsite in pursuit of a patch of grass.

'Yes, of course I know Thayer. He is my horse,' Talon said. Thayer snorted and shook his head. 'How do you know Thayer?'

'I just told you,' Roan snapped. He breathed out a cloud of smoke.

Thayer nickered loudly and slapped his tail on his hind.

'So, you know him because he is famous?'

'I knew the knight that rode Thayer,' Roan said. 'He was a famous knight himself. He and Thayer have some stories they could tell.'

'You knew my father?'

'Your father?' Roan choked. 'You're the son of Great Graer Telmache?'

'I'm Talon Telmache?'

Roan looked at him as though seeing him for the first time, then shook his head. 'No, I don't see the resemblance.'

'King be damned!' Talon said.

'I heard he met a girl from Hexon and settled with her and had a son. Now, you're saying that you're that boy?'

'How did you know my father?'

'He's a hero, boy!' Roan said. 'Any son of Graer would know at least that.'

'I can't believe you found my horse.'

'Your father's horse…if ye who ye say ye is,' Roan said. 'Is he?'

The horse nickered.

'I am,'

'Thayer is a knight's horse,' Roan said. 'Only a knight can ride him.'

'You're not a knight!'

Roan eyed him, 'Sages enjoy special privileges. Knowledge boy, knowledge.'

'Shut up about knowledge. Let me out of this thing so Thayer and I can be on our way.'

Thayer stalked off whinnying.

'He don' seem te agree,'

'He's not the same, since…' Talon bit his lip. He looked down at the ground.

'Tell me ye story, and if I like it. I'll get you to Rivon,'

'Where's that?'

'It's the closest village other than Weston. I'll hire a mercenary to escort you home.'

'I'm not going home,'

'Not my business after Rivon.'

A wolf pierced the silence with a long howl. The fire crackled as the dim golden glow illuminated their faces. Talon sighed. Currents of light grey overcast clouds swept across the misty sky concealing the sun. A cool wind whistled loudly through the mustard grass.

'My story starts, well…Alright… It starts with a girl,' Talon said.

Roan grinned.

8

THE CALL

A bee buzzed around the room loudly for a moment until it landed on the window sill. The room returned to silence. Blithe's eyes followed the insect as it explored the windowsill in strange patterns. Any distraction from her thoughts were welcome. She was anxious to hear back from Hexon Falls. She was anxious to hear back from one person in particular – her grandson. He was so much like his father, that it scared her sometimes. *Goat sack fools!*

She adjusted her weight in the comfortable wooden chair. The red velvet cushions laced into the seat and the back added tremendously to the comfort. They were in a large room in one of the castle towers, near a man-sized window that overlooked the castle courtyard, and beyond that the city of Terron, and beyond that the Terron Woods, and beyond that Hexon Falls, her home.

The chair next to her croaked. Nycie slept with her head tilted backwards, her mouth wide open. The woman was as beautiful as her daughter, who lay a few feet away fast asleep on the bed breathing shallowly. Katrina's long golden curls fell to either side of her on the white pillows underneath her. Her sheets were the royal crimson, with the royal family's golden phoenix, wings spread wide as if about to take flight.

Both Darringer women slept deeply. Both were exhausted from the trauma they had suffered in recent days. She knew she should focus on them for now, but her thoughts kept wondering towards Talon. Something was wrong. *Where are you?*

One of the giant polished-wood double doors creaked ajar. Princess Maya slipped into the room. Even grieving as she was, the women appeared majestic. Her light blonde hair was neatly tied into three tiers that rose above her by a foot or so. She wore an elegant blue bejewelled dress that puffed out from the knees down. She glided to the other side of Katrina's bed.

'How is darling Trina doing?' she asked, swallowing a sob. She lifted a handkerchief to her face and dabbed at her eyes.

'She's still struggling to breath,' Blithe said. 'The healer'll be back soon. Perhaps he'll tell us more.'

'You saved her life Blithe,' Princess Maya said. 'We... couldn't thank you enough. I know Calren... would... be so grateful.'

Her voice broke and she cried softly.

'Kat grew up in my house as much as in Nycie's. My son and her were very close.'

'Talon right?'

Blithe nodded.

'How is he? He must be distraught?'

Blithe looked up at her through her grey-blue eyes.

'I shouldn't have left,' she said. 'My men assured me they had Cal and Trina covered. I would never have...'

'It doesn't matter now,'

The crystals on the chandelier above Kat's bed chimed as a warm breeze swept through the room. The wind carried animated chatter from the courtyard below. There was a large market set up there for traders from all over the land to sell their goods.

The door creaked open more widely. A tall, muscular man, just past his middle years entered the room. He had light grey blond hair with black and grey streaks, and a matching, neatly trimmed beard. His brown eye scanned the room as he strode to Princess Maya's side.

'Your Majesty,' Blithe said standing to bow. She kicked Nycie's leg hard.

'Wha!...' Nycie said she looked around the room and then jumped up. 'Y-Your Majesty.'

'Greetings my good ladies,' King Warrick said nodding. 'Sister, what happened? I came as soon as I could.'

'Oh Warrick. It was terrible. Th-they were everywhere. Then they took him. They took our boy and stabbed poor Trina.'

'Barbarians?' he said. 'You're sure?'

'As sure as anyone can be of anything Your Majesty,' Blithe said.

Nycie sobbed silently. 'They did this to my baby. To the Prince.'
'What happened?'
'After the ceremony, they attacked with a large force, probably three hordes at least,' Blithe said.
'Three hordes? You're familiar with military talk?' King Warrick said. Princess Maya hugged him, and buried her face in his shoulder.
'My son is the late Captain Telmache, hero of the Battle at the Border,'
'It is an honour to meet you then,' the king said.
Blithe nodded. 'There were three war lords. One of them was Drag'a…'
'The son of Bragar?' the king exhaled. 'Why would he break the truce? We had peace for once!'
'He wants his brother back,' Blithe said. 'This is a kidnapping, and his brother the ransom price.'
'The ransom?' The king shook his head. Bells echoed in the background.
'I hate to think of what they are doing to my baby,' Princess Maya said, looking up at King Warrick with teary eyes. 'We'll pay the price wont we?'
There was silence in the room. Princess Maya scanned everyone's face.
'We will wont we? She repeated.
'Your majesty,' Blithe said. 'In all likelihood he is already…'
The king shot her a look that stopped her in her tracks.
'He's what?' Princess Maya said. 'What was she going to say?'
'He wants to kill your line of succession… as punishment.' Blithe said. Everyone stared at her with wide eyes.
The king said nostrils flared. 'Brandil!'
A thin man dressed in the royal crimsons entered the room. 'My King?'
'Assemble the Generals, now,' he said. He let go of Princess Maya. 'Excuse me ladies.'
Blithe and Nyclementia bowed.
The two men stormed out of the room. The door shut loudly behind them. The three women took their chairs around Katrina in silence. A dark cloud hung over the room, filled oddly with the happy and excited sounds from the market below. *War again?* The people below were blissfully unaware of how their lives would once again be changed as their worlds were flung into the dark fog of war, spreading fear and despair across the land.
'You think he's…,' Princess Maya asked. She couldn't finish the sentence.
'Don't think about that now,' Blithe said. Her eyes locked on to Princess Maya's. 'There is always hope.'
Princess Maya's lip quivered. Her large brown eyes filled with tears.
'Our role is to hope. To be strong. Not for our sakes, but for theirs. They may not come home. They know that. We know that. But for them to be

strong, requires that we be strong. For them to have hope, requires that we have hope. If they believe there is hope they will fight to come home.'

Princess Maya nodded and dabbed at her eyes.

'He will find a way to come home to you, and to his loving wife who longs for him, and to his beloved people who fight for him. He will come home.' Nyclementia said. 'He has to.'

Blithe eyed her friend out of the corner of her eyes. Her husband and son did not come home.

Princess Maya let out a loud cry and put her hand on her mouth. A tear streaked down Nycie's face.

Kat blinked and wriggled under the blankets.

'Baby? It's your mother,' Nycie said grabbing Kat's hand.

'Mummy?'

'Yes, darling.' She said.

'W-where's…,' Kat's voice broke. Her tea-green eyes opened revealing a pool of tears. 'Where's C-Calren?

Princess Maya sobbed loudly. Kat turned to look at the woman, her face racked with pain. Kat broke out into tears muttering under her breath.

'No, no, nooooo,' she whispered in between her cries.

The door creaked open again. This time a short balding man, with white hair entered the room. He wore a white robe with a crimson phoenix insignia on his left breast.

'Ah, Princess Katrina, you're awake,' the man said. 'I am Master Janis, your healer. This is my healing apprentice, lady Karys.'

Kat turned away and squeezed her mother's hand.

'It's okay baby,' Nycie whispered to her daughter. 'It will be okay.'

Princess Maya took Kat's other hand. The women cried together silently.

'You sustained dangerous injuries, very dangerous indeed, even life-threatening were it not for the primary care given to you,' Master Janis said. 'Which one of you administered this?'

'She did,' lady Karys said.

Blithe nodded.

'Very impressive,' Master Janis whispered.

'This is lady Blithe Telmache,' the princess said. 'She saved Trina's life.'

'Lady Telmache? *The* lady Telmache, as in the founder of this infirmary? Mother of Captain Graer Telmache?'

The other women's heads all turned to look at Blithe. The news was enough to suspend their sobbing. Blithe continued staring out of the window, her eyes lost on the treeline that led home.

'Well ma'am it-it is an honour and no wonder her royal highness is alive!' Master Janis said. He turned to Kat. 'You are very lucky indeed that the greatest healer in the history of the land was...'

'I am not lucky,' Kat snapped.

'Yes, your royal highness,' said Master Janis. 'I didn't mean to...'

'How will you proceed Master Janis?' Blithe asked.

Kat blinked and licked her lips. 'I'm sorry.' She continued to sob quietly.

Master Janis proceeded to talk loudly moving to Katrina's side.

'Why, might I ask did you ever leave the Royal Service? You were the Chief Healer were you not?' Lady Karys asked slinking up next to Blithe.

'My grandson,' she said. 'I stepped down to look after my grandson.'

'Of course,' lady Karys said. 'And where is he now?'

Blithe stood up and turned to look at them all. 'I would like to return home immediately. I assume Katrina will be alright Master Janis?'

'Well, yes Ma'am,' Master Janis said. 'She will most certainly make a full recovery.'

'Then I take my leave,' Blithe said. 'Ladies. Look after her. Kat, I will send Talon your love.'

Kat frowned. 'Don't!'

'Excuse me?' Blithe said.

'I hate him!' Kat shouted.

Before anyone could blink, Blithe had glided across the white-marble room.

'Be careful of the words you use young lady,' Blithe said. 'There is not an army in all the kingdom, King, Queen or Princess be damned that will stop me from undoing my work if you insult my grandson again.'

Kat turned away from her, her faced twisted in pain.

'That boy loves you. And I don't mean some fleeting fool love or some romantic storybook love. Real love. And that's more than you deserve,'

Everyone's jaws fell to the ground. There was a stunned silence that pierced the room.

'It is high treason to-to threaten a member of the royal family.'

'Arrest me or move out of my way,' Blithe said sharply.

Lady Karys stepped back.

'Don't mistake me girl,' Blithe said turning back to Katrina. 'I will never tolerate insolence from someone he cares for so deeply. That boy adores you girl, and you will do well to honour his friendship with some understanding and respect. Good day all.'

She turned on her heels and stormed out, slamming the door behind her. Anger radiated off her. Her skin boiled and her temple throbbed. *How dare that spoilt girl hate my boy!* She blew a stray strand of grey hair out of her face and made her way along the enormous hallway past the tall windows letting in the white light of midday. She passed the King, Brandil and another elderly man dressed in military uniform. The king looked up at Blithe as she passed and nodded. She nodded in return.

'Make the call general,' The king said loudly, almost at Katrina's door. 'We're going to war.'

9

THE LADY OF THE CANYON

'We've been traveling for days now,' Talon complained. 'How much further?'

'How ordinary,' Roan said exhaling a long jet of green smoke which filled the air with a soft hint of mint. He clenched his teeth around the end of his pipe and shook his head.

'Ordinary?'

'Never mind,'

'When do we reach this place?'

'Patience,' Roan said simply.

Talon clicked his tongue and frowned, but he obliged. They continued to ride in silence, their surroundings shrouded by a thick fog that clung to the air around them. So thick was the misty veil that Talon could hardly see five steps ahead of Thayer. The grass hills had given way to arid terrain mostly a dusty brown with patches of green and orange scattered beneath the horse's hooves.

Most of the trip had passed in silence. Talon had done most of the talking, or at least attempted to do so, but Roan's answers remained ever cryptic or worse simplistic. Talon's thoughts were focused mainly on how to escape the fate Roan had for him: to send him home in shame with some mercenaries. Thoughts of facing Kat's parents made his stomach knot. Thoughts of facing his M'ma gave him a cold chill.

Thayer paused pulling Talon out of his reverie.

'What's wrong old boy?' Roan said while patting Thayer's neck.

The horse snorted. Warm steam spirals floated from his flared nostrils.

'Easy, Thayer,' Roan said. He frowned into the distance. Talon tried the same, but only saw the same grey wall that haunted them in the latter part of their trip.

'Is something wrong?'

'Keep very still and stay quiet,'

'Why?'

Roan nudged Talon in his injured gut with his elbow sending a shock wave of pain through his body.

'You...' Talon began, but his words were lost in his throat. Someone stepped out from the grey veil. A tall figure draped in dusty brown robes that resembled the earth underneath them. Talon followed the glint of light from the sharp spear tip down to the tanned hand that held it firmly.

The only distinguishing features were the figure's eyes. A golden brown pair of eyes stared out at them. The eyes darted across Thayer, then Roan and then came to rest on Talon. There was an agedness to the eyes, as though they had seen too much. The outlined face should have been older, more wrinkled, but were smooth.

Roan spoke in a foreign tongue, a fluid, almost musical sounding language. There was silence for a moment. The figure moved the spear in an intricate pattern. All around them robed figures emerged with their spears lowered towards them. Roan continued speaking calmly to the lead figure, the only one whose spear was not aimed directly at them.

Talon clenched fistfuls of the back of Roan's robes to stop his hands shaking, but there was nothing he could do about his racing heart or his teeth clattering. The silence was deafening.

'Come Amara. No need for the theatrics,' Roan said. 'I just need a moment of your mother's time. My companion. He is wounded and lost. Perhaps I could hire Skahla to escort him home.'

'Who is he?' A husky voice replied in English from behind the robes. She had a strong accent.

'Is that a woman,' Talon whispered in Roan's ear.

'A Young village boy from the North-West,' Roan replied, ignoring Talon.

The golden brown eyes searched Talon once more.

'Why is he injured?' Amara asked in her husky voice.

'Bar-' Talon began, but another nudge shut him up mid-word.

'Traveling accident,' Roan said. 'He is rather clumsy and very foolish.'

'Why are you so determined to see his safe passage back home?'

'I owe his father a life debt,'

Talon exhaled through gritted teeth. Sweat sprouted across his brow and he doubled forward. The lead figure spoke in the strange language and the others disappeared within seconds, swallowed back by the fog.

'Follow me to Ashrah's Gate,' Amara said as she disappeared into the foggy veil. Roan ushered the snowy steed forward, and he obliged. Thayer kept a moderate pace so that Amara remained a few steps ahead at all times.

'Who was that?' Talon asked.

'Amara, Fal'a Skahla,'

'Fall Skull?'

'Fal'a Skahla, it means, the closest translation is Leader of the Deathbringers. She is a captain of the Skahla, a warrior clan who dwells in the Rivon Canyons.'

'She?'

Roan glanced back at him with a stunned look on his face.

'What?' Talon said.

'They are a formidable force, and their leader Lady Esandra, is short tempered. Let me do the talking. And no matter what don't speak.'

'But, I can tell her...'

'No!' Roan said through gritted teeth.

'If they are so strong they can help.'

'With your suicidal quest?'

'It's not suicidal, it's honourable,'

'Many people mistake stupidity for honour. Don't make their mistake.'

Talon clicked his tongue, and they continued in silence. He stared at the back of Amara's head. A woman was a captain of a group of warriors. Kat would have loved to meet someone like her. He wanted to meet her without her wanting to kill him. There were so many questions he would ask. They continued for fifteen minutes before Amara stopped. She raised a strange whistle and the sounds of gears began sounding behind the grey curtain of fog. A draft sucked the fog backwards into a large paved square revealing giant black gates opening to allow them passage into a large city.

Five hundred meters to their left stood a large building with spears hanging on the walls. A retinue of warriors glad in the dusty brown robes appeared around them once more.

'The horse and your weapons,' Amara said.

Roan jumped off the horse and then carefully helped Talon off. The dismount sent another shockwave of pain throughout his body, but he breathed deeply and tried to ignore it. Someone escorted Thayer out of sight and others took their bags, Roan's pipe and his staff. Amara had to remind him that it was a weapon. He let go of the staff reluctantly.

'No trust of the old anymore,' Roan said loudly.

Amara responded in her native language and then said something to the other warriors. They folded in formation around Roan and Talon and then nudged them forward. Amara led them through the streets of the village. Talon couldn't make out as much as he would've liked but he kept his focus on putting one foot in front of the other at the pace dictated by Amara's long strides. A warrior kept poking Talon in the back when he slowed his pace too much, which was often.

'For King's sakes, the boy is injured.' Roan said. He then spoke in the language of the region. The warrior made to strike Roan, but Amara whistled and the soldier froze, then stood at alert. She appeared next to Talon, the same height as him, and spoke in the fluid language to the warrior.

He bowed and said, 'I...Are...Sorry.'

Talon turn to speak to Amara but she returned to the front of the column and they continued on their way, through paved streets in between rectangular black stone buildings. They entered another large open area and then stopped suddenly at the edge of the cliff of the canyon. Talon felt a chilly draft from below sweep up. It was strong but not strong enough to break the fog. The refreshing wind was welcome to abate some of the heat, and to deter the sweat on his brows. The sound of gears working again and the sound of a large chain also echoed off the canyon edge. When it stopped a large wooden platform stood judge beyond the edge. Amara stepped onto it. Talon was nudged forward gently onto the platform. When they were all on it. A wrinkled hunchback of a man pulled a leaver and the platform descended at an alarming rate. Talon stumbled but was caught. He looked up to find Amara's eyes staring into his. She helped him upright and then stood back. Talon caught glimpses of structures and walkways extended across the canyon. It was hard to believe what he had seen. The scale of it.

The platform came to a stop and they continued into what appeared to be the canyon wall. They entered a large hall with guards on every door. These guards wore black robes with dark hoods. They stopped before a large black iron door carved with intricate scenes of some long forgotten battle. Two large torches on each side of the door cast a ghoulish orange light over them all. But the whir grey light of day penetrated the hall from angled slits carved into the ceiling.

Amara removed her hood, and the other warriors did the same. Amara's long black hair fell across her shoulders. She had a round face with soft features and tanned skin. Talon caught himself staring.

'Don't even think about it,' Roan whispered.

Talon looked at him eyes wide.

'She'll kill you,' He said.

The cold guards on either side of the large black iron doors pushed them open to reveal another large hall, smaller than the previous. This room was flooded with light from a large glass dome carved out from the canyon wall. Orange light shone from torches lit all around the room. Guards lurked in the shadows around the hall as well, their black robes blending in to the black stone walls behind them. At the centre of the room stood a few steps which lead to an elevated throne. A tanned middle-aged woman with haunting sapphire eyes sat in a luxurious black dress. She was barefoot and the dress revealed substantial cleavage and her bare arms and legs. Talon had seen nothing like it. The dress was very flattering.

'Roan Sage of the Cerion Valleys,' the woman on the throne said in a melodious voice. 'A face I thought I would never see again, because I vowed that if I did...'

'Mother,' Amara said.

The woman looked at her daughter and rose from her throne.

'The boy is injured,' she said.

'Is that why you let this traitor back into our city? An injured boy?' She shouted. She grabbed Amara's face forcefully. Then kissed her. 'Ever clouded by emotion daughter.'

'Who are you boy?' She said turning to Talon.

Talon looked at Roan.

'He is a village boy...'

Lady Esandra was quick. She closed the gap and slapped Roan loudly. Everything fell silent.

'I asked... the boy,'

Talon looked at Roan again. His cheek was red where her hand had made contact.

'Don't look at him,' Lady Esandra said. 'Speak your truth.'

'I - I am Talon Telmache,' He said.

'Telmache?'

'Yes,'

'As in THE Telmache, Hero of Heron Hill?'

'Yes,' Talon said. Roan nudged him in his ribs. 'Yes, ma'am.'

'So tell me young Telmache, what brings you to my realm?'

Talon leered at Roan out of the corner of his eye. Roan shook his head ever so slightly to avoid detection. Talon mumbled and stuttered, confused as to what to do next.

Lady Esandra, brought her beautiful aged face close to Talon's, 'Well?'

'I am on a quest... to... rescue... Prince Calren,' he said.

There was a moment of deafening silence, and then the entire room burst into laughter. Lady Esandra chortled audibly, her dark curls bouncing on her shoulders. Her arms wrapped around her middle. The warriors around the room rumbled with laughter in the manner Talon thought statues might.

'I'm telling the truth,' He screamed. He scanned the room. The only one not laughing was Amara. She frowned at him. Roan simply shook his head with disappointment.

'I hope for your sake you are,' Lady Esandra said suddenly, void of all laughter. 'Why would the prince need to be rescued by you? He is in the safest place in all the world.'

'He was taken a few days ago,' Talon exhaled.

'Taken? Impossible. He has an entire battalion of elite knights protecting him,'

'He was taken in my village. He married my best friend.'

'The Princess Katrina is your friend?'

'Wait, you know Katrina?'

'Yes, yes. All the nobles met the future queen,' Lady Esandra said swatting her hands above her head as if swatting away a pesky fly. 'They're safe, recently married.'

'Kat, - Katrina is dead,' Talon choked. 'And they took Calren.'

'Who?'

'The barbarians,' he said. The room dropped a few degrees.

'No barbarians would dare enter our kingdom, let alone be found so deep in land,'

'You must forgive my companion,' Roan said. 'He's full of these stories of wild fancies.'

'I'm telling the truth,'

'We'll see,' Lady Esandra said. 'For now, you will remain in the fortress as my guests, of course, while we verify this story.'

'Of course,' Roan said.

Lady Esandra shot Roan a foul look. She muttered something in their native tongue and the shortest warrior leapt from his post and bounded out of the room.

'Amara, dear, why don't you show our guests to their rooms,' Lady Esandra said. She turned and left the hall through a side door, and was followed by her entire retinue.

Talon watched the door close behind her. It felt as though his heart had fallen into his stomach. He slumped his shoulders and stared at the door as if doing so would magically bring the Lady of the Canyon back.

'Come,' Amara said.

Talon spent most of his free time sleeping, mainly on his back. If he moved around too much the pain would jolt him awake. Both he and Roan received large and elaborate rooms within the fortress. There was much to explore, from the intricate wall carvings depicting epic battles. Not to mention the fact that the entire fortress was carved out of the side of the canyon wall. The breadth and intricacy of the designs fascinated him, but it was also the very thing that led his eyelids to betray him.

It was a messenger at his door that woke him from his sleep. White moon light shone through a window at sharp angles and formed a bright square on the lavish rug next to his bed. Talon blinked away his fatigue, and pulled the door ajar without a word.

'Dinner will be served in one-hour sir,' the young girl said. Her head faced down.

'I'm not really that hungry, thanks though,' Talon said.

The messenger blocked Talon from closing the door. This made the girl's cheeks turn a shade of magenta, 'The Lady of the Canyon, *requests* your presence sir.'

'Fine,' Talon said, succeeding this time to close the door.

Fifty minutes later another knock at the door alerted Talon that it was time for dinner. It was Roan, dressed in an ornate chestnut robe with gold stitching forming patterns on both plackets and cuffs. He escorted Talon to the dinner hall, where the bottom of a long rectangular dinner table had been set for four. Talon and Roan sat across from Amara and Lady Esandra sat at the head of the table.

Lady Esandra wore a long black dress, low cut enough to reveal her ample bosom. The dress clung to her figure. Her long black curls were tied back neatly. Amara's outfit surprised Talon. She wore a flattering lilac dress she was clearly uncomfortable in. She kept trying to adjust the dress around her hips to give her more manoeuvrability.

Roan placed a firm hand on Talon's shoulder before the boy sat down ahead of Lady Esandra.

Amara watched this interaction silently and smirked.

'Please, sit,' Lady Esandra said as she herself took her seat.

Immediately attendants stepped forth from the background to lay down a drink and place an odd dish before them. It looked like a pink worm that was over cooked.

Everyone dug in, while Talon hesitated, preferring rather to watch the others eat the odd morsel.

Lady Esandra asked Talon to tell her stories of his village. That was a request he could oblige, and he did so willingly, with Roan's foot to guide him under the table when he veered off the appropriate path.

The young boy was further bolstered on by the sounds of chuckles coming from Amara. A break in her otherwise stern features. Talon thought she had a magnificent laugh, a soft sigh. The conversation distracted him enough to eat the strange food, which he enquired after, once he realised what he was eating. The women seemed only too willing to indulge his curiosity.

'Why so quiet Roan?' Lady Esandra said, after a long bout of laughs.

'Just pondering my lady,' Roan said serenely. 'The food however, is delicious, without a doubt. Thank you for spoiling us.'

Talon and Amara exchanged smiles as they chewed their food.

Lady Esandra, caught the exchange, 'Do you have a great love in this wonderful village of yours Talon Telmache?'

'Ye-,' He paused, and choked on his food. Roan slapped his back which helped. He swallowed hard and took a deep breath before croaking, 'No.'

'Such a handsome young boy?' Ey Amara, is he not handsome?'

Amara leered at her mother before focusing he eyes on her food.

'You speak so highly of Princess Katrina,' Lady Esandra said. 'It's a wonder such a handsome boy wasn't engaged to her long before she became a princess.'

Talon coughed silently. Amara looked up at him briskly her eyes curiously scanning him, before she returned her gaze to her food.

A warrior entered the room dressed in their usual garb. Lady Esandra gave him the signal to approach. He whispered in her ear and then he left the way he came.

'My men have dispatched our Sand Hawks to all the villages and towns in every direction asking after your barbarians,' Lady Esandra said. She rose. Amara and Roan rose as she did, but Roan had to lift Talon from his seat. 'Forgive me, I am tired and have a few matters to attend to before bed.'

'I should leave too,' Amara said, fidgeting with her dress. She performed signs and the girl from earlier appeared to lead them back to their rooms and ensure they had everything the needed.

A week had passed without news. Talon had not seen Amara again. Sofi, the girl attending him, told him that she was on patrols. 'A Fal'a Skahla is an important role,' Sofi kept repeating. This meant Talon was forced to explore the town on his own. He visited the market place, the local bakeries, the various shops, and travelled on the platform that ascended and descended up and down the canyon wall.

On one such day, the skies were a perfect blue and at the top of the canyon Talon could see for miles in every direction. For the first time he became aware of the massive bridge spanning the Canyon. The largest gates he had ever seen blocked passage across the bridge. These gates had sizeable turrets on either end with room for many an archer to make camp. He wondered what was on the other side.

Sofi came running after Talon who was watching Skahla train. Their movements were so fluid and graceful; unlike anything he had seen.

'Master Telmache,' Sofi yelled from a distance. Her robes blowing in a gust of wind.

'Hiya Sofi,' Talon said. 'What's wrong?'

'Lady,' She took a deep breath and doubled over, waited a moment and then continued, 'Lady Esandra, needs to see you.'

'Where is Roan?' he asked.

'Already with… her,' she huffed.

'Lead the way,'

They walked at a brisk pace through the crowded streets filled with towns people going about their business.

'How strong are the Skahla?' Talon asked out of the blue. The thought had occurred to him moments before.

'Strong?'

'Yes, uhm, are they the best soldiers in the land?'

'Yes Master Telmache, they are,' she said finally.

'What about the King's Knights?' he asked.

'No,' she replied.

Talon glanced at her sideways. She was shaking her head.

'No?'

'No,'

'What are you saying no to?'

'King's Knights no strong. Skahla, strong,' she nodded firmly as she said this.

They were silent the rest of their trip. They joined Lady Esandra, her guard, Amara and Roan in her large fortress hall. An ominous silence hung in the air.

'Young Telmache,' Lady Esandra said. 'You brought grim tidings which seem horribly true.'

'You found them?' he asked.

She nodded and then glanced at her closest body guard.

'Does this mean we can go after them?' Talon asked. Everyone looked at him with wide eyes.

'Go after him?' Amara said.

'You want to go after an entire Barbarian Horde?' Roan said, clicking his tongue. The sound reverberated off the stone walls.

'Yes,' Talon shouted. 'Someone has to do something. Isn't he going to be the next king? Doesn't that count?'

'We've sent a sand hawk to the capital,' Lady Esandra said.

'Sending hawks? What for? We know where they are don't we? Let's go and get him.'

Heat emanated from his cheeks and he clenched his fists tightly. Roan watched him closely but he didn't move a muscle.

'Mind your tone with the Lady of the Canyon,' Amara said.

'My tone? So no one will help?' Talon asked. 'Fine, what are we going to do?'

'We wait for word from the capital,' Lady Esandra said. 'Then we decide.'

'Are we free to leave?' Talon asked, cutting her off.

Amara frowned and leaned forward. The rest of the guards took a step forward.

Lady Esandra used one hand to stay Amara and the other to signal the guards to stop. 'You are free to travel as you may young Telmache, but I am curious. What will you do?'

'Go get him,'

It was difficult to tell but Talon would have sworn all his savings that the room went quieter, so much so that he could hear the flickering of the flames on the lamps around the room.

'No you won't,' Roan said.

'You can't stop me,' Talon said.

'I will,'

'Why prevent him from his quest?' Lady Esandra said with a grin.

'There is no coming back from this quest. Trained warriors would not accept such a quest, and now a fledgling proposed to make it?' Roan said.

'Travers would have done it,' Talon said.

'The Travers you know, is a myth boy,' Roan said. 'No sane person would do this. Follow sound counsel and await news from the capital.'

'No,' Talon said. 'I'll leave in the morning.'

He turned and stalked off. Back in his room he paced thinking about their reactions, or lack thereof. He screamed and shook his head. A knock sounded at the door. He paused a moment considering who it might be. He doubted he could keep his composure with anyone who wanted to talk him out of his decision.

'Master Telmache?' It was Sofi.

He opened the door unable to find the words or common decency to speak politely so he remained silent.

'Lady Esandra, says she and her guard will see you off at the King's Bridge tomorrow at dawn.'

'Why cross the King's Bridge?' He said. 'That's not the way I came.'
She shrugged her shoulders and shook her head.
He nodded and bid her goodnight.

Though the orange sun had barely risen, it was already considerably warm. The native russet robes he wore were deceptively cool. When Sofi presented the robes to him earlier that morning initially he was rather reluctant.

He was unsure of what to expect, but he packed his bag, and headed out to the King's Bridge entrance, guided by Sofi. The residence of the town had not risen yet, but waiting for him at the bridge, was Lady Esandra and her guard as promised. Sofi, shorter than Esandra went to stand next to her lady.

To Talon's surprise, Roan rode out from behind them upon Thayer. The sage held the reigns of chestnut mare, which walked out alongside Thayer.

'Saddle your bags to old Jezza here,' he said.

'You're coming with me?' Talon asked.

'Don't get excited,' he said.

Talon couldn't help beaming.

A thin mist crept along the stone streets weaving in between their feet. The canyon heat was palpable. Talon swept away a few beads of sweat from his brow, and turned to Lady Esandra. Bowing deeply, he thanked her for her hospitality and apologised for the previous evening.

'Go well young Telmache,' she said. The bright morning's orange glow gave her a majestic appearance.

A crow cawed somewhere above them. The black bird contrasted starkly to the clear blue skies, not a cloud in sight. His M'ma would have told him that was a good omen. He smiled and bowed again.

After readying Jezza, he mounted her. It was a completely different experience to ride a horse who obeyed instructions.

A shout came from his right as the King's Bridge Gate rolled up slowly. He searched the horizon to find a group of riders approaching on horses, all hooded Skal'a. Their leader stopped in front of him. Amara unhooded herself.

'Me and my Skal'a are coming with you.'

Talon blinked wildly unable to speak. Amara dismounted and approached her mother who was already yelling in their native tongue. Amara replied equally audible. She cut her mother off and said something final and returned to her horse.

'Let's go,' she said.

They ushered their horses forward and entered the gates as though entering into the jaws of a giant beast.

10

The Concept of Hell

Katrina shifted her weight on the back of her black colt. The animal pranced about at her movement.

King Warrick pulled alongside her and calmed the animal. 'Forgive, young Arden, he is an eager thing.'

'No, he's perfect,' she replied through gritted teeth.

'Your wound?'

She grimaced, placed her hand over the area and took a deep breath.

'The pain fades eventually. It never fully vacates, but it fades.'

'I don't know if I want it to,' she said. A pigmy owl hooted as if in agreement. The sound reverberated through the trees swaying gently in the wind. The mid-morning sun light trickled through the trees casting abstract shadows on the grass. The smell of fresh mint and wet bark filled the air of the Western Woodlands. Katrina had never seen it before, but Calren had told her many stories of how he had come hunting here with his uncle. They were amongst his fondest memories.

The beams of light turned the forests green branches of the tall oaks into light lime. The creatures of the woods sang, whispered, slithered, chirped, and char-charred. It was a wondrous choir that created a deep sense of peace to the place. It was hard for her to imagine this was the same world in which monsters existed. She peaked out of her eye to check that the king was not looking and then she dabbed at the tears under her eye.

Ahead of them and behind them, the soft crunch, crunch, crunch of the soldier's boots and the horse's hooves were the only sounds out of place. The army trampled over the moss and wet grass that had grown over the dirt road. Just before noon, they came to the end of the Western Woodlands, which opened on to a hilly grassland which slowly descended into a shallow valley to the east.

A burly man decorated with ribbons and medals of every imaginable colour, blew a horn which paused the march of their company. A message was shouted along the column until it reached them and a soldier, part of the king's personal guard shouted, 'Half an hour!'

The same message was shouted behind them and continued along the lengthy column to the rear. The king helped Katrina dismount. He was as gentle as he could be but she still bit her lip in pain. She was surprised at how accommodating he was. She had nearly committed treason the way she defied the king's wishes for her to remain behind with the women at the castle. She had outright refused him publicly and was yet to apologise for that. She doubted that she would.

The king's servants set a tent without any side walls and a thin hessian roof. They set a table and a magnificent spread of teas and delicacies. The generals, commanders and Lords joined the King and Katrina at the table. They waited for the king to serve himself and then they joined him.

'Eat something,' he whispered to Katrina.

'I doubt I would be able to keep it down, your Majesty,' she replied softly in his ear.

He nodded and smiled through the white and brown beard growing over his face. It was a shock to be the only woman sitting at such a table. She wanted to ask the king about it but thought better of it. Rather she sat in silence while the men around her chatted animatedly, or had hushed conversations to themselves with those sitting closest to them. The king's guards distributed at all corners and sides of the tent along the table eyed everyone suspiciously.

A horn sounded announcing the arrival of a group. The horsemen stopped shy of the tent and dismounted. Two of the king's guard approach the soldiers and removed any weapons they had on them. They were King's Knights, finely dressed with shiny armour in the colours of the kingdom. Talon would have given anything to be seated where she was now. He would have given anything to be in the presence of the knights who he so admired. They seemed as impressive as he made them out to be, proud and stately.

'Your Majesty, Lords, Generals and Commanders... and uh... and Lady,' the lead knight said. Clearly Katrina's presences threw him off his game. 'I present to you Lord Anwir of Weston.'

Everyone fell silent.

'My Lord,' King Warrick said. 'I won't waste your time since we have but none to waste. Please explain how it came to be that an entire Barbarian Horde roamed free in my kingdom without my knowledge.'

A gaunt man with hollow eyes cast glances across the table and licked his lips. One of the knights pushed him forward. 'Y-your majesty, Lord, Generals, Commanders and-and- and Lady,' he said.

'You shall address Princess Katrina, as her Royal Highness,' King Warrick said. His voice boomed sending nearby birds in the trees squawking away from the nearby treetops.

'F-forgive me your Royal Highness,' Lord Anwir said bowing deeply in Katrina's direction. 'Your majesty.'

The man glanced up to see whether his apologies had landed and when he noted they had not he continued. 'I deemed it necessary to preserve the-the sanctity of the truce you established between the Barbarian Hordes and our Kingdom. As such, I allowed our-our guests to stay in Weston upon the strictest condition that they behave themselves.'

'Have you ever known Barbarians to behave themselves my Lord?' the King said. He placed his elbows on the table and cupped his hands as if about to pray.

'I hoped your majesty...'

'You hoped?' the King chuckled deeply. 'My Lord, you hoped, I wonder what it is you hoped for indeed.'

'P-please your majesty, I,'

'Enough,' the King said. 'May this be a warning to any Lord who deems, or hopes or thinks they know what is best for this kingdom absent of my consult. Lord Anwir Dolion, Lord of Weston, by the authority vested unto me, I hereby place you under arrest pending a trial where you fault and causation in the Hexon Massacre and the kidnapping of his Royal Highness Prince Calren.'

'No, my king. Pray please forgive me,' Lord Anwir pleaded, falling to his knees. He crawled toward the king, but did not make it far, before the knights scooped him up and dragged him off as he flailed wildly in the air. 'My lords, my lords, help me my lords.'

The table remained silent. One or two of the men coughed and most deliberately avoided eye contact with the man as he was dragged off.

'Captain Shondir,' the king said. The lead knight stood at attention. 'Ensure you question the Lord of Weston thoroughly.'

'Yes, your majesty,' the dark skinned man shouted. He stamped his foot and marched off after his men.

Katrina exhaled finally unawares that she had been holding her breath the entire time. She looked down to find red marks where he nails had bitten into her palms.

'Pay attention my dear,' King Warrick said. 'Leading is an impossible challenge for the best of us. Each move is calculated; each might be your last.'

Katrina blinked at him emptily. He smiled and rose, all the Lords rising as he did. He stalked off trailed by his personal guard. The lords waited a moment and then took their seats and began chatting animatedly once again.

The campfire crackled loudly. The warmth of the fire licked Talon's back under his blanket. The rest of his body remained icy cold. He looked out into the empty grasslands in the distance tracing with his eyes the place where the dim orange glow of the fire met the darkness of the tall yellow grass.

A fat black beetle buzzed as it fell awkwardly on the edge of the sand before the grass and kicked its legs wildly to flip the right way round before disappearing into the grass. Talon closed his eyes ignoring the sound of shuffling behind him.

His eyes opened suddenly. Talon was unsure what had woke him, or why his heart was racing. Perhaps a dream he could not remember, or a nightmare. He had lost track of what time it was, but heard voices chatting behind him. Roan and Amara.

'Why will you not train him?' Amara asked.

'Why are you so emotionally invested in this village boy?' Roan asked.

They both sat in silence for some time.

'His spirit,' Amara said. 'It's different.'

Talon could feel Roan's long tentative stare piercing Amara's even though his back was turned toward them.

'Young men should not die for the wars of foolish old men,' Roan said.

Again, they fell silent listening to the fire crackle and the wind whistle through the grass.

'If he cannot defend himself, from Barbarians or old fools in power, then we will go to the slaughter any way. No?' Amara said.

Roan exhaled loudly. The wisps of smoked travelled lazily on the breeze passing over Talon and then dissipating into the darkness.

'If you will not teach him, I will,' Amara said.

'You're in love with him,' Roan said.

Silence fell again. This time Talon was sure it was Amara starring daggers at Roan. The two were playing a strange game, where Talon did not understand the rules, or the game.

'Be careful, that your attachment, does not get you killed,' Roan said, exhaling again.

"Be careful, that your lack thereof does not kill you,' she replied. There was shuffling. Then the sounds of footsteps crunching on the dry grass.

Roan huffed loudly and clicked his tongue. Then silence apart from the soothing licks of the flame and its fading orange glow. After a few minutes Talon drifted off to sleep once more.

'Get up boy,' Roan said loudly.

Talon had lost all track of time. It was still dark, but the faint hint of sunrise lingered on the edge of the night sky.

'What's going on?'

'We are breaking camp,' Roan said. 'Long way to travel.'

'A few more minutes,' Talon said.

'Knights don't sleep in you fool,' Roan said.

Roan pulled his blanket off of him. A wave of ice cold air splashed over him.

Talon yelled and shivered. The cold seemed to have seeped into the painful scare in his abdomen.

'Okay, fine.' Talon said, struggling up and shivering.

Everyone else was already dressed and on their horses.

'What is wrong with you people?' he said.

'Here's some breakfast,' Roan said shoving a hot cup of stew into Talon's hand.

Talon blinked desperately at the fatigue in his eyes. Try as he might his mind struggled to start up. Roan hosted him up with his breakfast and placed him on Thayer. He jumped up himself and ushered Thayer forward.

Talon looked back at the camp and noted that it looked as though they never stopped there for the night.

Later that morning, shortly before noon, they stopped. The flat grasslands gave way to hills with a slight incline. The mountains loomed in the distance. The rest of the party dismounted, and made preparations for lunch.

Talon made to join them, but Amara pulled him away. 'Come with me,' she said.

They walked about a mile away from the camp to an isolated part on the other side of the hill.

'What are we doing here?'

'I am going to teach you to be a warrior,'

'Really?' he said. He had a large grin on his face.

'This will not be easy,' she said.

'I can do it,'

'Even so, it will not be easy,'

She tossed him a thick wooden stick. He flailed trying to catch it, but ended up dropping it in the sand.

'To begin, we must determine how much you know and how much you do not,' Amara said. 'Attack me.'

'What?' Talon said. 'I can't, hit a girl. That would be dishonourable.'

'How much more dishonourable then, if she beat you to a pulp,' she replied. 'Either you attack me, or I will attack you.'

Talon did not move.

Amara moved towards him. Talon turned to run, but before he could take a step a sharp pain hit his shoulder and the momentum sent him spinning to the ground.

'Don't ever turn your back to an enemy who has a weapon aimed at you,' she said.

'Now get up and try again, and this time do not flee, like a coward.'

Talon got up and they went again. He did not run, but he flinched every time she tried to hit him. She beat him every time, and after an hour of abuse, they returned to the camp.

'Interesting training session?' Roan chuckled when they returned. The men joined in on the laughter. One of Amara's soldiers handed Talon a plate of food, which he accepted in a foul mood.

'We have a lot of work to do,' Amara said. She looked as though she ate a raw lemon whole.

They continued to ascend to the base of the mountains in the distance over the next few days and for the next few days Amara continue to attempt to train Talon with very little positive result. This frustrated both of them which was visible in the distance they kept from one another when they were not training. What further irritated both of them was how much glee the situation gave Roan and the other warriors. Much of the campfire banter in the evenings was at Talon's expense.

A week later, they were sitting at the campfire enjoying a meal and the party was making its usual fun. Talon had a swollen cheek, which the group made fun of.

'Silence!' Talon said after another round of jokes at his expense.

'The next person who makes a joke…'

'You'll what?' Roan asked. 'You'll expose your bottom for another great walloping?'

The men erupted into fits of laughter.

Talon, grabbed his sparing staff, lifted it above his head and swung, for Roan's head. Roan dodged the blow and rolled along the floor, stood gracefully out of harm's way. The warriors cheered. Again, Talon swung madly at Roan's mass, but he blocked the blow with the outside of his forearm, stepped towards Talon and punched him in the chest so hard he fell on his back completely winded.

Talon writhed in the dirt near the fire, gasping for air. His eyes were wide with awe.

'I am not some girl too in love with you to hurt you, boy,' Roan said.

The campfire went silent.

'You will never be a knight because you are too cowardly,' He said. 'Isn't that what Drag'a said? Be a good coward and crawl back to the hole you came from and save us all the trouble of dying on your fool's errand.'

Talon's face burnt red hot. He rolled on to his stomach, got on all fours and then with sheer rage hoisted himself up.

'Your girlfriend is dead, boy, so you fighting a lost cause. Even if she wasn't dead, she wouldn't be yours anyway,' Roan said. 'That not only makes you a coward, but a stupid one.'

Talon roared and rushed Roan. Within seconds, he was hoisted up, and thrown over Roan's shoulder and slammed head first into the sand.

'If you take this long to get up, when fighting a barbarian berserker, I might as well kill you now. It will be a mercy killing,'

'Stop,' Amara shouted. She had her spear in hand.

'Stay out of it Amara,' Roan said.

'No,'

'Then I'll be forced to teach you a similar lesson to your new love interest,'

The rest of the warriors rose. Amara signalled them not to intervene. Talon coughed and rose to all fours again.

'Come save your coward,' Roan said. He kicked Talon in his side sending him on to his back in agony.

Amara spear stabbed at Roan's head for a kill shot, but he twisted out of the way, Amara continued to strike, twist, strike, with her spear, and for all her moves, Roan, dodged or parried the blows with ease.

'Perhaps, love does not conquer all,' Roan said, dodging another fatal blow to the chest. 'You can't even land a single blow.'

Amara screamed and increased the intensity of her attacks. Finally, Roan found an opening after a thrust of Amara's spear, and smashed the side of her head with the back of his fist. She fell to the ground and the others drew their spears. Again, Amara signalled them not to intervene. She jumped up from the ground, picked up her spear and circle Roan. Talon jumped at Roan from behind, as Amara thrust her spear at an opportune moment, Roan danced out of the way, grabbed the back of Talon's shirt and yanked him backwards so that Amara's spear tip just grazed his chest.

He threw Talon to the ground and kicked Amara's spear into the air, swept her off her feet, caught the spear, and held the spear tip to Amara's throat, while placing his boot on Talon's back.

No one breathed, except for Talon who groaned, and Amara who breathed heavily.

'You're both dead,' Roan said. He took his boot off Talon, and stuck the spear into the ground and lifted them both up.

'I'll teach you to defend yourself,' Roan said to Talon, 'But you won't like my methods. In fact, they may be akin to the concept of hell. If you are not able to bear this burden, I suggest you go home now. If you are prepared for this, then I suggest you go get some sleep, because you will need it.'

Roan, grabbed his pipe, dusted it off, stacked it with a minty tobacco, and traipsed off into the night.

11

THE MOUNTAIN

Talon ducked as Amara swung her sparing staff across the place where his head had been. She turned and then jabbed the staff at his centre mass tipping him over into the dirt. She moved toward him and jabbed again this time directly for the centre of his face. Talon cringed. He raised his arm and closed his eyes.

'Get up,' Amara said. 'That is enough for today.'

Talon opened his eyes to stare down the thick end of the ageing wooden staff.

'If this was a real spear and I a real enemy…'

'I would be dead,' Talon said. 'I get it.'

'I do not think you do,' Amara said. She fetched her neatly folded brown robes off a nearby boulder.

Sweat beat down Talon's face and his body ached from the various places Roan had slammed him into the ground the night before. His ego took the bulk of the beating. The sounds of laughter from last night and his whole life echoed in the recesses of his mind.

He stood up and dusted the dirt off his clothes as best he could. Dirt and sweat smudged his brow and he could taste the granules of sand on the tip of his tongue. The first rays of dawn peeked out from the edge of the horizon. Amara threw him his coat and the two returned to camp in silence.

Breakfast was waiting for them. Roan's cold blue eyes followed them when they entered the camp. Amara's men cast furtive glances at Roan when they thought he was not looking. The previous night's events had cast an uncomfortable blanket of tension over the group.

'We ride out in five,' Roan said with his pipe hanging loosely between his lips.

Five minutes later, when Talon tried to mount a horse, Roan stopped him. 'Your training has begun young Telmache.'

'What does that mean?' Talon asked.

'Your wish has come true. I'll train you, but only on the condition that you obey my every command, my every instruction. If you cannot do this, I will stop your training immediately, remove you from this party and return you to your village.'

Talon blinked up at Roan, his right foot halfway into the stirrup.

'Here your bags. You carry those the rest of the trip and try keep up,' Roan said. The sage threw Talon's heavy bag on the floor. It clanked loudly on the hard ground.

Amara's soldiers looked at her. Her face was red, but she said nothing.

Roan clicked his tongue and Thayer begun to trod off sending Talon falling backwards.

'Keep up, boy!' Roan shouted. The rest of the group began following Roan, each person giving Talon an apologetic look as they passed.

'You can overcome this,' Amara said passing him.

Talon hoisted his bag over his shoulders and began to jog after the horses as best as he could. He stopped, then walked, then continued jogging. An hour of this and the straps of the bag had begun to chafe his shoulders. His lungs seared from the cold air entering and exiting in rapid succession.

After another hour, Talon lost sight of the group completely. He was wholly relieved when he eventually found the group sitting around a small fire having lunch. He hobbled awkwardly into the temporary camp and fell on to his back without removing his backpack. He panted like a wounded animal.

'F-finally, lunch,' he huffed.

'We've been here for two hours already on an extended lunch. We ride out in five minutes,' Roan said.

'I- I only just got here,' Talon said. 'I haven't eaten anything yet.'

'Food is for those who can keep up,' Roan said. 'But you can have some water.'

The sage threw a flask down next to Talon. He gobbled it up and asked for more. Roan chuckled and gave the order for everyone to keep marching on.

'Don't take too long,' Roan chuckled.

Talon closed his eyes hoping for a short break. He started awake, only to realise the sun was setting. They had not waited for him. He struggled up like the old tortoise he had once seen in the meadow back home. A quick scan of the horizon told him he had fallen far behind. The plains ahead were desolate. He started on the path after the others, the only landmark the lonely mountain. With a heavy sigh, he made his way in the direction he watched the group leave. He had no torch which made it difficult to see where he was going by the time darkness set in. He continued through sheer will dragging his feet along the shrubs and dirt. Hours passed without Talon able to see five metres in front of him. It was not until late in the evening when in the distance he saw the flickering of a campfire. It was still miles off, but the darkness helped him identify where he needed to go.

That single beacon of light in the distance gave him hope. He kept moving slowly towards it, and slowly it grew brighter and larger until he could hear the soft muttering of the warriors, and anxious neighing of the horses.

He entered the camp and once again fell to the ground exhausted. Someone gave him a bowl of warm soup. Talon had never smelt anything so wonderful in all his life. The warm liquid filled his belly. He felt sheer glee as he wolfed down the food. He was given another bowl and he emptied that too, licking the bowl clean afterwards. He drank water so fast it spilled over his cheeks and wet the collar of his robes.

'Now then,' Roan said. 'We spar again.'

'I can't,' Talon said.

'I thought so,' Roan said. 'Then you and I return to your village tomorrow.'

There was silence around the campfire. The flames crackled loudly and the yellow-orange glow cast a grim light on Roan as he puffed away nonchalantly on his pipe.

Talon breathed heavily, then wriggled out of his bag's straps, and rose slowly. His entire body ached, either from the beatings of the previous day or from the agony of his horrific hike earlier that day. He assumed a fighting stance or his closest approximation of one.

Roan attacked without warning. Talon tried to duck or dodge the blows but failed. After five gruelling minutes he lay on the ground winded, his nose bleeding and his eye swelling shut.

It was Amara who called for the fight to stop when Talon's left eye was swollen too badly. Amara helped him back to where his bag lay. She covered him in his blanket. He was far more exhausted than he was in pain, so despite the aches across his body, when he closed his eyes he fell off to sleep almost immediately.

It was ice-cold water splashing over him, that shocked Talon awake. 'Time to go spar with Amara,' Roan said. 'She will teach you how to move your body during combat.'

Roan nodded at Amara, who helped Talon up. He faired just as badly with Amara as he had with Roan, but when the sun rays passed the horizon, she called the session to an end. They returned, had breakfast, and once again, the group left Talon to hike after them. They repeated this pattern day after day, for almost a week and each day Talon grew slower. He returned to the camp at night later each night, and after sparing with Roan only got the bare minimum hours of sleep.

After two weeks of this unending torture, Talon limped into camp, dropped his bag and headed straight to Roan. Someone held out a bowl of stew for him, but he slapped the bowl away. The warrior cursed loudly.

'I want to go to bed so let's get this over with,' Talon said.

Roan squinted at him for a moment and then nodded. They took up their position, Roan started towards Talon. Without flinching, he dropped his arms to his side, stared at Roan dead in his cold blue eyes, willing the old sage to hit him hard enough to knock him out. He closed his eyes and waited for the blow, but it did not come.

Talon blinked. 'What's wrong old man? Hit me and be done.'

Roan walked away and took a seat. 'You have learned the first lesson.'

'What?' Talon asked.

'In a fight, you cannot be afraid to be hit,' Roan said. 'For now, we will rest here a day or two to allow you time to recover.'

The group received news of the break well. There was a buzz of chatter, drinking, singing and dancing that evening. Even Amara sang a song after some coaxing from her tribesmen. It was also the first time Talon caught Amara smiling at him form across the campfire. It was in response to the tumultuous round of applause.

Talon turned in early. He covered his head with his blanket and fell asleep. His rest was uncomfortable. Whenever he moved, the pain would wake him. He would doze off again, accidentally move, and be woken up by the sharp prang of pain surging throughout his body. This continued well into the next morning.

The rest of the warriors went off to find a local hot spring, others went hunting and the rest remained behind performing odd tasks such as sharpening their spearheads, stocking up on wood, repairing their shoes. Roan was not in camp for the two days, but Talon spent the entire time sleeping or trying to.

On the afternoon of the second day, Amara dragged him to the hot spring. She undressed before him, so he turned around stunned. She laughed.

'You village folk are modest,' she said. 'Have you not seen a woman naked?'

'N-no. That is reserved for a husband and a wife!'

'Well, I am in the water,' she said. Talon turned slowly and indeed she was. He joined her wearing his undergarments. They spent the afternoon in the water talking about their different upbringing, their families and debating who were better fighters, the Skal'a or the King's Knights. At sunset, they returned to the camp, they ate, they sang, they danced and they shared stories as a group. Talon was not sure if it was the warm spring water, Amara's company, the rest he took over the previous days or the fact that Roan was no longer amongst them, but he felt in better spirits than he had in a long while and the aches in his body were slightly less painful than before.

The next morning, Roan woke Talon with icy water once again. 'Back to the routine, I am afraid.'

Blithe Telmache heaved the last wooden box on to the back of the large wagon. The tattered yellow wood wagon creaked under the weight of the load. The wagon swayed from side to side like a drunk miner after final call dancing to some music only he could hear. The breeze blew soot and dust into the air around them. Months had passed since the barbarians attacked. And in all that time it still felt as though the heat of the flames emanated off the stone walls, those which remained standing.

The rest of the town was reduced to ash and rubble. Blithe scanned up and down the empty street. The only sound was the haunted whistle of empty winds winding through the broken crevices of Hexon. Blithe shook her head, climbed into the driver's seat of the wagon and ushered the horses towards the town's exit.

She passed through the once bustling town square, now an ancient ruin, devoid of life or laughter. A shadowy figure emerged from the mist. Peyton Price, a beautiful girl, out of place in such a place of devastation.

'Hiya Peyton,' Blithe called, waving.

'Mrs Telmache,' she said. Her wide eyes indicated she was surprised to see anyone about. 'Where are you going?'

'I was going to ask the same of you,'

'Me?' she said. She glanced over her shoulder. 'I had to get away.'

'From?'

'My mother, her wailing. Watching her smother my, my da's clothes,' she said. She raised a flask to her ashen lips and took a large swig. Her face twisted as she swallowed. She looked up at Blithe and followed the older woman's eyes to her hands, 'Faers.'

Blithe frowned, 'Best I be on my way.'

'You didn't say where,'

'Exactly,'

'Can I come?' Peyton asked. She raised her eyebrows. Blithe was certain those eyes could enchant even the most frigid of men.

'No,' Blithe said. 'Good day Miss Price.'

Peyton jumped up on the wagon while it was in motion. She shuffled into the seat next to Blithe, who pulled the wagon to a halt.

'Get off Miss Price,' she said.

'No,' she replied grinning. 'Not until you tell me where you are going.'

'Talon,' Blithe said.

'Huh?'

'I am going to find my grandson. He is missing and no one in the forsaken troll of a village cares. Not a one. Now if it is all the same Miss Price, I would like to go.'

'I like Talon,' she said. Blithe blinked at the girl. 'I like him a lot actually. He is not a pest like the other village boys. Doesn't have those greedy eyes.'

Blithe opened her mouth, but words would not escape her tongue.

'I think I would make a fine daughter-in-law if he ever managed to ask me, but I doubt he will ever move on from Kitty Kat,' she said. 'Your boy has it bad. Worst I have ever seen.'

'You need to get off,' Blithe repeated.

'What if I did come?' she said. 'You're getting on in years, and could use someone to run the errands around camp.

'It's not safe,' Blithe said.

'What do you mean?'

'For a – for a young woman. On the road. It's not safe,' she said.

'Nonsense,' Peyton said looking ahead. 'You're a slightly less younger lady, it's not safe to let you travel on *your* own.'

Blithe sighed, 'For goat sakes girl, go fetch a bag and meet me at the entrance of the village.'

Peyton jumped off the wagon and dashed off.

'And you tell your mother what you up to, hear?' Blithe shouted.

'Ep sag Tauir,' Talon said. He hopped from one boulder to the next. 'Ep sag Tauir.'

The phrase was burned into the back of his mind. *I am Talon.*

He was unsure which was worse, learning the barbarian language or his rigorous training regime. His muscles still ached, but it was a dull ache. He had even come to enjoy it. Earlier that morning he had woken before the rest of the camp and thrown a flask of ice water on Roan to wake him. He had spent a long time running from the old Sage who chased him unrelentingly. He was surprisingly fit for an old man.

His punishment was that he had to carry Roan's bags for the day as well as his own, but it was worth it. The horses were just a few miles ahead of him these days. He tracked their movements along the ridge where they ascended the mountainside steadily. A month had passed since he stood up to Roan and in that month much had changed.

They had begun to ascend the mountain. The greens and browns gave way to yellow, then orange, and now white. While ascending the mountain the temperature plummeted. The first visible sign of the cold was the mist he exhaled every time he breathed. This was new to him. It looked as though he were smoking a pipe like Roan. The sunshine gave way to a miserable overcast sky perpetually rumbling. It had not snowed yet.

Amara had begun to teach him about movement during their morning training sessions. *Combat is like a river. It always flows and so must you.* Her voice echoed in the back of his mind most of the day. At lunch, he would perform strength training with Goron, one of Amara's warriors. He was built like a rock and his skin was as hard as the hide on a horse. Talon found himself lifting rocks above his head, climbing trees when there were those available, holding various positions which burnt his arms, or his legs, or his chest or his back depending on the position Goron instructed him to hold. Each day was something different, and then a few days later he would begin the routine again.

While Talon jogged behind the horses, he practiced Barbarian phrases and pronunciation. To him it sounded like he was gagging and hissing incoherently. Roan understood him which was a positive sign, however he doubted a barbarian would be convinced by his language skills.

In the evenings, he first ate, chopped wood, practiced his Barbarian phrases for the day and then proceeded to spar with Roan. Each night Roan beat him, but nothing as severe as that first night. Each day he would rise without prompt and when he wasn't pranking Roan he headed to a secluded field near the camp to practice before Amara joined him yawning and stretching the sleepiness away.

On one particular morning, he rose earlier than usual. His fellow travellers slept silently forming small mounds under their blankets. A few feet away the horses remained just as silent, not moving a muscle. The campfire had gone cold. A chill set in the air giving him goose bumps on his forearms and the back of his neck.

The sky was especially dark, giving no indication that the sun would rise any time soon. He felt an eagerness to continue his training. There was a particular sequence Amara had shown him that he wanted to master. In part, he wanted to impress her, in part, he wanted to prove to himself he could do it. He snuck out of camp, his feet crunching through the thin layer of sleet. He found a small open area, which was as flat as he could hope for along the jagged mountainside.

Talon looked up and watched the small flakes of snow slowly fall to the earth in silence. He marvelled at what he saw. His first snowfall. He thought of Kat and her adventurous nature. She would love to see the tiny white flecks sink through the air defying the pull of the earth. He closed his eyes and thought of her a moment more. He gave himself that moment, then he blinked and allowed his anger to fuel his training.

Amara joined about an hour later. It grew lighter revealing the various greys of the overcast sky. It was strange to not see the sun, especially considering how high they were. Talon could see far into the horizon the way they had come.

'Are you ready?' Amara asked.

He nodded.

She circled him, her knees bent, her sparing staff twirling in her hand. She jabbed at him, he moved the way she had shown him and parried the blow.

'I would love a staff,' Talon said. He watched Amara's hand, her feet, and her body as he was instructed to do.

She feigned with her feet and made to swipe the staff across his face, but he ducked and rolled away from danger, back onto his feet and swung around to anchor his eyes on her once again, scanning for signs of her next move.

'A weapon is an extension of you. It is only for those who have mastered hand combat.'

Amara struck again, he saw an opening like she previously described. He set his feet, locked the staff between his side and his arm, and he shoved her at the moment she was most off balance. Amara stumbled backwards, but the staff remained in his arms. There was a round of applause. The entire camp was watching them and most were cheering him on.

He grinned at them, blinking wildly. He turned his focus back to Amara, but her fist smashed into his face sending him to the ground.

'Never take your eyes off your enemy,' she said.

He grunted trying to ignore the stinging of his jaw from the floor. He tasted the familiar metallic tang of blood in his mouth and spat it out. Amara offered her hand.

'Enough for today,' she said. 'Back to camp.'

They returned in silence. Roan stayed behind. He was watching the fight too.

Several more weeks passed, and each day Talon improved his movement, his hand combat, and eventually his spear training. Eventually, at the peak of the mountain, atop all of the world, Roan, excused Amara from Talon's morning training sessions and took over himself.

He returned Talon's father's sword to the boy. It felt much lighter in his hands than he remembered. Further to this Roan had him train in his undergarments. First, Roan showed him the various sword stances, then the sword defences and finally the sword attacks. Talon was annoyed by how much thinking was involved in fighting. He had never been the best of students.

He trained every morning in his undergarments and then again in the evenings. He continued to hike through the thickening snow behind the horses, carrying his heavy bag and leaning against the blistering wind that felt like tiny daggers stabbing at his exposed skin. He began to have a basic grasp of the barbarian language. He scared the people in his party by uttering harsh phrases in the guttural language. Roan watched this disapprovingly but made no effort to intervene. It was practice.

Another week later they began to descend the mountain as they made their way toward Bregfurjen, the land of the Barbarian hordes. One evening, after training, the warriors asked the sage to tell them a story.

'What story shall I tell?' he asked them.

'Tell them the story of this mountain. The story of how Travers Cailyn rescued Queen Talia from Bragar himself and the Giant Wolves,' Talon said.

The warriors approved. They chatted animatedly in their own language and stared at Roan with wide eyes.

'Very well,' he said.

'Not too many years ago, Queen Talia was escorted home to her father's castle, because the old Lord was deathly ill. She and her sisters buried him that autumn. The king was away at war and could not be there personally himself, so he entrusted the one he loved the most to his most decorated knight, Travers Cailyn, the Commander General of the kings' Knights.'

The camp did not make a sound. Only the fire crackled in the emptiness, the flames hardly generating any heat. Talon looked over at Amara who was as captivated by the story as her men.

'Bragar had caught wind of the Queen's father's death, some say he had something to do with it. No one knew, but Bragar and his most fierce bezerkers ambushed the queen on her return to the capital. There was a fierce battle. Travers was separated from the rest of the knights and barely escaped with his own life. When he returned to the queen's carriage, it was a gruesome scene. All his men were dead, the barbarians were gone and so was Queen Talia. It seemed all was lost, but not for Travers. He had made a solemn vow to protect the queen with his life. So he pursued the barbarians who fled into these very mountains to make a hasty retreat to their fortress in Bregfurjen. It was on these haunted mountains, that they heard the howl of the Giant Wolves. The ravenous pack descended upon Bragar and his men and in the chaos Travers was able to rescue the princess and escape with her to a cave where they hid from the wolves. They survived months in that cave...'

'That's not how the story goes,' Talon said. 'They returned immediately to the capital and Travers was heralded as the greatest hero in the kingdom.'

The camp all broke out of the spell and glared at Talon.

'That is how the fools who know nothing tell it,' Roan spat. 'This is what actually happened.'

'No,' Talon said. 'I have the book here.'

'Don't believe all that you read you fool. Storytellers love to embellish.'

'And you? How do we know you are not embellishing?'

'Shall I tell my version or not?'

'Tell it,' Amara said before Talon got another word in. Her warriors agreed.

'Very well. The pair hid in the cave where Travers nursed the injured queen back to health. He made preparations for them to descend the mountain. During this time Travers and the queen developed a strong friendship that would last till the day they died.'

Talon shook his head but said nothing.

'Travers left the cave to draw the wolves away from the queen who fled. Travers fought the wolves on the great ice lake at the top of the mountain and used the ice to disorientate the wolves long enough to strike fatal blows to the alpha. Travers left a scar on the face of the smallest of the wolves, a pup. He dragged himself out of the ice water and made his way to the queen. The king had many enemies, so he hid the queen under the guise of her being his wife, and together they made the long journey home. Along the way Travers became horribly ill, but as fate would have it, they came across kingsmen who recognised the queen and Travers. They were rushed back to the capital where the Head Healer of the day saved his life.'

'What? No way' Talon exclaimed. 'That is completely wrong. Talon rode the queen back into the capital on a nobleman's horse to the triumphant cheers of the citizens.'

'Do you hear yourself?' Roan asked. 'Where did he get the horse?'

'I don't know. He is Travers Cailyn!'

Roan's face went red. His cold blue eyes grew colder if that were possible.

'Well, thank you for your version, I prefer my own,' Talon said. He crossed his arms.

There was an uncomfortable silence around the campfire. Roan got up and walked off cursing under his breath. The silence continued as everyone looked at one another.

In the distance, loud and piercing, a gut-wrenching howl echoed through the mountain range.

12

THE WOLVES

The camp erupted into a buzz of activity. The hair on Goron's furry forearms stood on the ends. In his panicked rush, he kicked over the pot of stew into the fire. Sparks exploded in every direction. One rogue spark caught the sleeve of Talon's cloak. He punched his arm into the wet and cold snow. Roan prepared Thayer's saddle with a speed Talon had not known him to possess. He slipped his pipe into the pocket of his green cloak.

'What's got into you all,' Talon asked. Getting back up. The smell of burnt stew and ash stung his nostrils.

Another piercing howl erupted, closer this time. The horses whinnied audibly.

'Are those wolves?' Talon asked.

Several more cries echoed the first.

'The giant wolves,' Amara said shoving Talon towards his things. 'Pack!'

He knelt down, frowning. The rest of the group scrambled their belongings into their bags as fast as they could. One of the warriors made to pack the spilled spot away.

'You fools,' Roan shouted. 'Leave it.'

The warrior looked at Amara. She nodded. They left the fire, the pots, and some of the other utensils. They focused on preparing their horses. Thayer was the only animal that remained calm in the fray. The other horses reared as their riders approached them. Some flailed their heads and flicked their ears. Others snorted inconsolably.

Talon threw his bag over his shoulders.

'Take that off,' Roan shouted. 'Ride Jezza.'

Talon approached the chestnut mare. She stopped the ground and whinnied. The horses smelled of weeks of travel. They needed a wash when this was all over.

'Easy girl,' he said holding his hand out to her neck. He patted her coarse flank gently. She was too jumpy for him to mount. Every time he tried, she reared. Roan came over and whispered into her ear, allowing Talon enough time to mount.

The rest of the group had similar struggles mounting their steeds, but with some assistance from Roan the party was ready to ride.

'Follow me in a single file. We descend the mountain as fast as we can, but the cliffs on the way down are treacherous. Stay close and move fast,' Roan shouted.

The wind had picked up and a thunder rumbled in the distance.

The cold wind stung Talon's face as he rode. He squinted but still could hardly see anything ahead of him in the dark. Each rider carried a flame torch, but the darkness was overwhelming. The thick snow made it difficult for the horses to move as fast as their rider's wanted. Roan rode Thayer, behind him Talon rode Jezza, then Amara and her warriors followed in single file on their horses.

They rode in silence. The wind shrieked in his ears. The party edged down onto a wide ledge on the side of the mountain edge. It appeared to be an old path, wide enough to fit two horses at a time. It was not as heavily snowed over as the mountain top from which they had just come. They had begun their descent. It was a day or two's ride to the base of the mountain as Talon understood it. He glanced off the edge to his left and only saw darkness. The spiralling white specks fell with increased purpose. Roan muttered something but the wind prevented Talon from hearing what he said.

'What are you doing?' Talon shouted after him. Roan ignored him.

Talon shook his head and looked back at Amara. He could see the fear on her face and the anxiety in her eyes. She looked at him without saying anything, but that said enough. He doubted he would hear her anyway. He was beginning to understand why they called these the haunted mountains. The wind shrieked like a troubled spectre. He shrugged his shoulders and turned forward. He focused his eyes on Thayer's pale hide. The white stallion navigated the rocks and the ice on the path effortlessly, while Jezza and the other horses slipped and stumbled along awkwardly. Talon had never been a fan of heights and now he hung off the edge of the world, on a nervous horse.

A peel of thunder erupted over the cliffs edge not too far from them. This sudden sound, scared the horses. Amara's horse stopped in its tracks and tried to back up into the other others. Her horse, kicked a rock off the edge of the mountain. Talon gulped at the ease with which the stone fell to its oblivion.

'Keep moving!' Roan yelled.

Talon ushered Jezza forward with her reins to keep up to Roan. They moved too fast for his liking along the path. It widend further, and levelled in certain places. This made it easier. They descended quickly along the mountain as it twisted and turned around and down the mountain side. A bark-howl erupted nearby somewhere behind them. The sound was deafening. It put to shame the wind and the thunder. The horses broke out in to a panic. Snorting, stomping and trying to kick their riders from their backs.

'Move!' Roan shouted over the wind. He sped up on Thayer and for a moment Talon lost him. Talon kicked Jezza on her side with his heel, 'Come on, girl!' He said. She complied.

'No matter what happens, don't stop,' Roan said when Talon caught up. '... Others,'

Talon frowned. *Tell the others?*

He turned and shouted the message as loud as he could. While looking back, he saw two red fires appear from the darkness, then sharp teeth and the last rider in their party disappeared into the dark.

Another fell silently off the cliff in what felt like an instant and then they too were gone. Amara signalled him forward.

'GO!' he shouted at the back of Roan's head. The old sage turned, to witness another member plucked off by a shadowy figure. All they heard was the feint growling, and gnawing, and ripping, and the agonising screams that pierced the silence for only a moment before that too disappeared into the dark.

Talon kicked Jezza in the sides. He flicked her reins, willing her forward. *Come on. COME ON!*

Thayer was faster than the other horses. Jezza heaved and huffed trying to keep up. Thunder exploded next to the cliff side followed immediately by a brilliant fork of lightning. The blue light illuminated everything in the dark as though it were the midday sun. Behind what remained of the group, an enormous wolf chomped at the tail of the last horse in the column. Talon swore he saw a scar across the lead wolf's left eye. The warrior screamed at his torch fell off the edge and he collapsed to the ground. The shadows swallowed the scene.

Talon could hardly believe the size of the beast. Its head was large enough to swallow half a horse whole. His heart drummed against his chest. He kept glancing at Amara who shook her head. She abandoned her torch, reached for her spear, leaned back and flung it behind her. A cry erupted and a white shadow fell from the mountain howling. The heavy snowfall swirled off the edge threatening to pull them all with it.

Amara was barely visible by the light of Talon's torch. The darkness almost had her. The ominous red embers of the front wolf's eyes appeared above Amara's head. Instinctively, Talon flung his torch at the wolf's massive head. The yellow-orange light hit the creature square and the torch burst into sparks. An agonising howl erupted from the creature and then silence. Amara was safe.

Roan continued mumbling in some strange language. Another flash of lightning and thunder erupted over the mountainside. It revealed the wolves had ceased their chase.

'ROAN!' Talon yelled. He did not respond.

Talon slowed down to level with Amara, 'Are you okay?'

'Don't stop!' she said. She was crying.

He could hardly see her in the flickering light of Roan's torch. 'You go in front of me,'

'No!' she said.

Roan stopped. 'Both of you, in front of me, now go!'

They swapped and rode on. Roan kept mumbling. His eyes were closed. Amara led the pack, then Talon and finally Roan. That was all that was left of a party of thirty of the finest warriors.

The fiery embers appeared behind Roan once again. The path twisted around a bend. They turned the horses in time, but one of the wolves, was too big, too slow. It cried as it fell off the edge and disappeared into the blinding blizzard beneath them.

Roan looked over the edge and nodded to himself. He looked forward to check that Amara was still fine. Roan shouted loudly as the red eyes appeared behind him once again. The largest lightning bolt struck the mountain top above them and the thunder shook the earth underneath them.

Roan open his eyes and he smiled at Talon. He nodded. Talon frowned. His heart was somewhere in his throat. The lead wolf's snarling muzzle reared for attack over Roan's shoulder.

'ROAN!'

'TALON!' Amara shouted. Talon glanced at her. Then above them to the right. Then back at Roan. He, Thayer and a few of the wolves, were swept off the cliff edge by a wave of snow.

The earth continued to shake. Or it was his body. He was unsure. Jezza ran for her life as did Amara's bronco. The snow wave crept closer and closer to Talon, sending everything in its path off the edge of the mountain. The sound rumbled and roared louder than anything he had ever heard. He focused forward. He screamed at the top of his lungs forcing Jezza forward at full speed. The mountain curved again ahead. Amara took the turn, and so did Talon. They escaped the avalanche and brought the horses to a stop. Talon jumped off Jezza who struggled for breath.

He ran back toward the edge where the white snow waterfall continued to flow over the mountain edge.

'ROAN!' he shouted off the edge. The wind, and the snow swallowed his cries. Amara gripped him and pulled him away from the edge. She pulled him to the wall of the ledge and held him there.

'He's gone,' she said. There were tears in her eyes as well. 'They're all gone.'

Talon slunk to the dirty ground. He burst into tears and shouted at the top of his lungs. His cries went unheard on those lonely haunted mountains.

13

THE BREGFURJEN

Amara and Talon entered the shadows of the woods. Large towering cedar trees rose in every direction obscuring the grey skies. The ground was littered with wet moss and emerald ferns. The tang of wet grass, mould and dirt reached his nose. A light drizzle pattered on the leaves of the trees around them.

They stopped their horses by a nearby stream trickling along gently, unaware of the nightmare of the last few days. They dismounted and filled up their water bottles. Neither of them had eaten a full meal in days. They had snacked on left-over rabbit meat and berries in their rush to get off the forsaken mountain that had claimed the lives of the group. For the most part rode in silence, reeling from the experience they had survived.

Talon leaned against the base of a tall tree. The bark pinched his back, but he ignored it. He closed his eyes and watch the scene of Roan and Thayer falling off the edge of the mountain. He remembered the smile Roan gave him before the fall. Did he know he was going to sacrifice himself for Talon? Why would he do that?

A woodpecker knocked on the trees nearby. Another bird answered the call in the distance. This brought him out of his reverie. He wiped away tears and made fists.

'We should find food and eat. Then we can decide what we do next,' Amara said.

'And what is that?' Talon asked.

'I don't know,' She said.

'Everyone's dead Amara. We should be too,'

'We're lucky, yes,'

'Luck? Luck had nothing to do with it. Roan saved us,' he said. 'He –We should never have been in those mountains. He tried to warn me.'

'He knew what we would be facing. We all did,'

'I didn't,' he said. He shook his head. The rain pattered away softly in the awkward silence that ensued.

'We can't stay here,' she said. 'This is the Bregfurjen. On the other side of this forest in that direction, lies the barbarian stronghold. They hunt game in these forest. Patrol it.'

'We should head home,' he said.

'Home?' Amara said. 'After all of this?'

'Yes, home,' he said. 'I miss my M'ma. Everyone is dead. What are we still fighting for?'

'Our prince needs us,' she said.

'And the two of us are going to rescue him from the barbarian fortress? We barely survived a mountain!'

She shook her head. She stood in front of him holding out her hand. The birds and insects fell silent. She looked up listening.

'What?' Talon asked.

An arrow whistled through the trees and scraped along Amara's cheek. She fell to the ground screaming.

Talon got up. Another arrow sunk into his arm sending him spinning to the ground.

He writhed in pain and yanked the arrow out of his arm. Blood trickled out of the wound staining his brown cloak. The horses neighed and snorted.

'Barbarians!' Amara shouted. She crept to the horses and pulled out her spear. 'Get up.'

She threw him a dagger, knelt and waited. A large barbarian warrior wearing a hog mask, rushed out the bushes wielding a large hand axe. He rushed Amara, she dove out the way, rolled and got back to her feet. He made for Talon who was still on the ground.

Talon rolled backwards and on to his feet, and ducked the swing of the axe. He shoved the barbarian backwards and took up his fighting stance with his knife. The barbarian jumped to his feet and roared before charging Talon again.

Amara threw her spear at the man, but he dodged the blow and struck at Talon again, he side stepped the blow, and saw and opening and jabbed the barbarian between his ribs. The mountain of a man backhanded Talon sending him to the ground, mounted the blow and readied himself for a kill shot to Talon's skull.

Amara pounced at the man and kicked him in his face. The barbarian fell to the side. Amara helped Talon up. His head spun as did the forest around him. He smelled the sickening smell of blood unsure if it was his or the barbarians. He was covered in it. He panted heavily. The barbarian jumped up raised his axe and mock charged them. They jumped. With another roar, the barbarian attacked again, both of them dodged, but the barbarian shoved Amara, who tripped over tree roots. The horses neighed loudly and kicked behind them. Talon found another opening at the barbarian's leg and slashed his dagger across his attacker's knee.

The barbarian growled and swung his axe at Talon's torso. Talon caught his arm. He kicked the barbarian in the middle and slashed across his chest, but missed.

The warrior stumble backwards, and Amara's spear tip clipped his shoulder. He made for her, but Talon rushed him. He changed directions mid-stride and instead swung the back of his axe and hit Talon across the head. Not with full power but with enough to send Talon flailing to the ground.

He heard Amara call his name, and the sound of clanking and grunting as they fought. His ears rung and he blinked wildly as he got up on all fours. He felt the wet leaves and the sticky mud on the palms of his hands and his knees. He heard his name again. Amara screamed, he jumped up shaking his head. The barbarian's axe had half sunk into Amara's shoulder and he pinned her against trunk of a tree. Blood rushed down her arm. Talon screamed and rushed after the barbarian. The warrior swung his arms as Talon approached. The boy was quick enough to roll out of the way. This afforded the warrior time to punch Amara square in the face. The back of her head hit the tree and she crumpled to the ground silently.

He ripped his axe from her shoulder at an awkward angle and swiped at Talon who crept up behind him. Talon went low, swiped at the barbarian's thigh and planted his blade deep. The barbarian roared, and grabbed Talon by the neck, hoisted him up and slammed him to the ground winding him. Talon's blinked widely gasping for air. The axe plummeted to slit his head in two. He rolled on his side. The axe sunk into the mud, he rolled back and stabbed the barbarian in the neck, again and again. The barbarian fell forward and roared splattering blood over his face. He yanked the knife from the warrior's neck and sunk it into his chest, then his side. His opponent collapsed on top of him with all his weighted winding Talon again. He took a deep breath and shoved the man off of him slightly and crept out from underneath him.

Talon crawled over to Amara who lay still. He put his hand on her face. Her skin was softer than he thought. She looked peaceful.

'Amara,' he whispered. 'Amara, wake up.'

Blood continued to stream out from her shoulder. The gash was deep. There was too much blood. He opened her eye lids, but there was no life behind them. She was asleep. She had to be.

'Amara,' he repeated. 'AMARA!'

He lifted her limp body and held her in his arms. He crept back with her and leaned against the tree trunk where she had been pinned moments before.

'Please,' he whispered over and over.

The woodpecker knocked on the trees above his head. Other birds chirped away. It began to rain, the rain pattered softly on the leaves. The forest was as peaceful as Amara who laid in his arms. Talon sat against that tree in a stupor for an eternity. His sadness was surpassed only by an unquenchable anger. He cried for her until her body went cold in his arms, and then he cried some more. Inside heat rose from a part of him he never knew existed. Some carnal place that wanted revenge that wanted to tear all the world down.

'You're beautiful,' he said to Amara's lifeless body. 'I was planning on telling you that when this was all done. Kat was beautiful too. You would have liked each other I think.'

A loud horn echoed through the forest. A chilling sound that sent birds scattered into the trees and made the hair on Talon's neck stand on edge.

A barbarian guard. This was only a scout.

Talon was going to die. He would never have the chance to avenge Amara or Kat. He would never rescue Prince Calren. He would never see his M'ma again or eat her wonderful cooking. He would die alone in these woods and no one would know. Roan would have died in vain, and so would the Skal'a who had bravely risked their lives to get him to this infernal land. He closed his eyes. He was tired. He was not sure he wanted to live in this world without Amara, without Kat. It was a world devoid of hope or happiness.

Was this what Travers felt when he waited to die? At least I will die the same way as my hero.

Disguise. Divert. Devise. *Those were the words the authors always spoke of when they spoke of Travers and his cunning plans.*

Talon looked at the barbarian sprawled on his face a few feet away.

Disguise. Talon had a thought. What if he wore the barbarians' clothes? He was almost the same height. Would the other barbarians approaching believe he were a barbarian? He looked at Amara's face and remembered her words. He didn't believe he would survive this next part, but for the sake of all those who sacrificed to get him here, he had to try.

He lifted Amara and placed her head gently on the ground. He kissed her forehead and said goodbye. He wished he had the chance to do the same with Kat.

Disguise.

He got undressed. Covered himself with mud and then undressed the barbarian. He put on the clothes and paused to throw up. He pulled the black furs over his armour and removed the warriors mask and placed it on himself. It stank of foul breath and sweat. He breathed shallowly. He looked at the naked figure lying there. He would not be able to explain it away to the others. He grabbed a rope from Amara's bag, tied it to both the horses' saddles and then wrapped the barbarian's legs.

Divert.

'Okay, Jezza and Izobella,' Talon said to the horses. He rubbed their necks. 'I need you to carry this goat sack fool as far as you can. You hear me?'

He smacked the horses on their flanks and they ran off in the opposite direction out of the forest. Talon picked up the barbarian's axe and cleaned it on his black sleeves. He wished he could see what he looked like. Wondered if it would work. If not, he would take as many with him as he could.

Devise.

He needed a plan. What was the plan? He needed to get to Bregfurjen Fortress. He scanned the ground and made his way to the brush where the barbarian had come from. He found a bag there, the bow used to shoot at them. His arm still stung from the arrow that had pierced his arm. He found a yellowing, ivory horn. He blew into the thing sending a shrill shriek into the air.

Here we go.

Talon's blood boiled. His stomach lurched as he waited. He readied himself in fighting formation just in case. He could barely keep his grip on the axe in his hands because they shook so much. He was soaked through to his skin because of the drizzle that continued to fall.

The brush shook to his right. A group of Barbarians slipped through in attack formation.

'Brahthurs,' Talon said in as harsh a guttural tone as he could, raising his axe.

Brothers. The barbarian warriors greeting.

'S'gul hathru?' The largest of the warriors said lowering his axe.

Good hunting? The right response was the same reply.

'S'gul hathru!' Talon uttered.

The barbarians cheered.

'Nas'thr,' the commander said.

Report.

'A'sru'gars!' Talon said. He pointed in the direction the horses had galloped.

Insurgents.

'Ep kuru ehyn,' Talon said.

I got one. He pointed to Amara.

The others grunted loudly in approval. The commander uttered orders quickly, too fast for Talon to hear. The commander ordered one of the warriors to report this to the fortress. Talon was about to speak, but the commander turned to him before he could and stared at him.

'Khar Al'a,' he said to Talon.

Go with?

Talon grunted the sign of ascent and banged his chest loudly.

The barbarian he was tasked to follow, slipped through the brush and Talon chased after him. It was working. He took one last glance at Amara's body.

An hour later, Talon and the other Barbarian, entered the famous black stone fortress of the Bregfurjen. Home to Bragar, Chieftain of the Bezoboar Hordes, the most despised barbarian in all the world.

Outside the castle were farm houses, and a village that looked similar to any that Talon would find in one of their own villages. In the courtyard to the fortress a rickety old wagon was loaded with figures covered in white sheets. Talon had never seen anything like it. This must be how they took care of their dead.

They climbed the jagged black stone stairs to the main hall where there was a crowd forming. He and his fellow barbarian stopped to see what the comotion was about.

'You fool,' a harsh gutteral voice said. The rest of the barbarians remained silent. 'The Great Chief gave me a fool for a son!'

Talon's heart nearly jumped out of his chest. Drag'a knelt before a fierce, much older barbarian.

'Apologies father,' Drag'a said.

Bragar!

Talon shook all over his body. He took a deep breath trying to calm himself.

'Apologies? You have pulled us into war boy! For what?'

'For my brother,' Drag'a shouted.

Bragar punched his son in the face, 'SILENCE!'

No one made a sound in the throne room.

'You,' Bragar said. He pointed to Talon. Talon's heart stopped a moment. He remembered himself and beat his chest in acknowledgement. 'Take the prisoner to the dungeon.'

Bragar looked down to his feet where Prince Calren lay sprawled, badly beaten, his face swollen to nearly twice its size.

'NOW!' Bragar shouted. Talon edged forward.

'Lord Chief, this brother must report insurgents,' Talon's fellow barbarian said.

'I gave him instruction,' Bragar said.

The barbarian warrior did not argue. Rather he bowed his head. Talon grabbed Prince Calren by his collar and dragged him away. The crowd parted showing where he needed to go.

'Hagthur, en uth Khar,' Talon said to his fellow barbarian.

Help and then we go.

The barbarian nodded, grabbed the other side of Prince Calren's collar and they dragged him off together.

The fortress had small windows near the high roof which allowed the grey light to enter. This was supplemented with flaming torches that cast a dim orange light in the dark halls. Barbarians moved to and fro in the castle. Only the women and the servants wore no masks. Talon was astounded at the beauty of the barbarian women. From the stories he was told they were described as ancient hags which called down curses on little children. They were not much different to the people of the kingdom in many respects. They went about their business, farming, raising their young, going off to war, and growing old.

They descended down a spiral staircase to the dungeons. There was one guard there snoring away in a chair. Talon's comrade, kicked the guard awake and asked for the keys. He pointed to the wall with his axe.

Talon grabbed the keys and led the way to the only cell left unoccupied. He opened the cell and allowed the other barbarian through to drop Calren off. He slipped his axe out of his belt, took aim and as the barbarian rose he swung the axe into the side of the barbarian's neck. He ripped the axe out and swung this time at his throat to silence him. They must have caused a commotion, because the guard shouted after them. Talon called for his help.

The guard appeared sleepy. He pointed at the other barbarian on the floor. The guard made to draw his axe but Talon was too quick. He lobbed the guards hand clean off. The guard yelled, but Talon broke his throat with the back of the axe shaft. He drew his dagger and he stabbed the guard repeatedly in the neck. The barbarian slunk to the floor gargling in his own blood as he did.

Talon stopped, took a deep breath and listened to hear if others were coming. It appeared as though the walls of the dungeon had done their job and muffled any sounds that may otherwise be heard.

He dragged the guard into the cell and placed him next to the other dead barbarian. He paced the cell staring at Prince Calren's limp, malnourished body. *How do I get him out of here? He looks half-dead. He won't be able to walk out of here.*

Talon cursed under his breath. *The white sheets. He looks half dead anyway.*

He rushed out of the dungeon. He walked calmly in the halls, towards the outside courtyard. He found the wagon filled with dead figures.

'Brahthur,' Talon said.

'Brathur,' the barbarian loading the dead bodies replied.

'Ep son'ner ehyn,' Talon said in the harsh guttural tone, pointing at a dead body.

I have another one.

'Var?' the Barbarian asked.

'Duhrn,' Talon said.

Down. Talon did not know the word for dungeon. He nodded back toward the castle.

The barbarian glared at him a moment and then shook his head. He threw a sheet at Talon, who thanked him. It took every fibre of Talon's being not to run through the halls like a mad man. He wanted nothing more than to be free of the place. He returned to the cell and everything was as he had left it.

'Prince Calren?' he said. 'Can you hear me?'

The prince groaned.

'It's Talon,' he said. 'I am going to get you out of here but I need you to stay very still. Pretend to be dead. Just don't actually die.'

Talon locked the cell with the two barbarians in it and threw the key in to another cell with an occupant. He wrapped Prince Calren in the sheet and left a slit for him to breathe through. He threw the prince over his shoulder and walked him out into the halls. Some barbarians stared at him as he walked past with a dead body hanging over his shoulders.

Calren groaned.

'Shhh,' Talon whispered.

He got to the wagon and loaded Calren in amongst the dead corpses.

'Ep sag ulhur tag,' Talon said to the barbarian loading the wagon.

He grunted angrily and shook his head. Talon stumbled backwards. *Barbarians don't show fear.* He pounded his chest and the barbarian did the same. The light drizzle started up again. Talon raised his hands and walked away and around the wagon.

There was no rider. He waited biting his lip thinking. Perhaps he would follow the wagon to its final destination. How long would that take and how long before someone noticed something was wrong in the castle?

As if to answer his question, the barbarian scout party he had encountered earlier entered the courtyard on horses with the naked barbarian mounted on the back of the commander's horse. He scanned the courtyard and Talon had to all but duck out of the way behind the wagon to avoid being seen.

That was too close. I need to go.

The commander would be reporting that there was an imposter amongst them. The barbarian loading the wagon, stopped and then entered the castle. This was it.

Talon's eyes were wide with relief. He jumped into the wagon, took the reins of the two horses and ushered them forward. They left the courtyard and entered the village with cobblestone roads and dark stone houses. Beyond that he came across the farms and farm lands were barbarian young tended to the fields and the animals. Once he had reached the outskirts, Talon ushered the horses forward at full speed, but the wagon was heavy and slow. He brought the wagon to a halt on the road near an open field and dismounted. He untied the horses and unhitched the wagon.

His hands were still shaking.

'Calren, I mean, Prince Calren.'

He rummaged through the bodies, panicking for a moment that he had left Calren behind, but a feint groan let him know the prince was still there. He unwrapped the prince who gasped for air. He blinked through his swollen eye.

'T-Talon?'

'Yes!'

'W-where's Katrina?'

'We have to go!' Talon said.

A loud guttural horn blew, different, more sinister, and louder than any other he had ever heard. The sound must have carried for miles. The sound echoed through all the world it seemed, once more and then again.

'The war horn,' Calren said.

'The war horn? We definitely need to go. Come on.'

Talon helped Prince Calren to his feet and then on to one of the horses.

'The forest is just up ahead and the fords beyond that. We can make it,' Talon said mounting his horse.

The war horn of the Bregfurjen blew once again.

14

THE COWARD

Talon and Prince Calren rode as quickly as they could, given the prince's condition. They broke into the forest soon after abandoning the wagon of dead bodies. Talon was unsure of which way to go but heading in the opposite direction of the barbarian fortress seemed like the best course of action.

'Do you know how to get back?' Talon asked over his shoulder.

'No,' Prince Calren said.

Talon ushered the horses forward.

The brush to their right rustled. They slowed down. Talon ripped the felid mask from his face and drew his axe. He was unaware until them how much he was sweating. Beads dripped off his forehead. The fur coat clung to his skin.

Roan and Thayer broke through the brush. Roan was hunched over Thayer bleeding from his head. He looked older than usual as though he had aged a hundred years since Talon last saw him.

'Roan?'

'Talon? Prince Calren?' the old sage said. His blue eyes were wide with disbelief.

'How are you alive?'

'Sages are very hard to kill,'

'What does that mean?'

'No time for that. Those war horns are for you,'

'Who is this Talon?' Prince Calren said.

'There'll be time for introductions later,' Roan said. 'Follow me.'

The three riders fled through the trees. They heard loud drums beating rhythmically in the distance. The horde was mobilised and on their heels.

They ripped through the brush. The leaves of low branches slapped at the faces. They ducked and dodged through the trees angling this way and that to avoid the trees and their knobbed roots. The drums echoed louder and louder still.

The barbarians had the advantage. They knew these woods well. The horses panted loudly and so did Thayer, scraped and bloodied as he was. The horse was tough and well trained.

The drizzle increased in intensity into a torrent. Talon had to wipe the rain drops out of his eyes every so often so he could see where he was going. Branches swished past him every so often. The horses' hooves thudded loudly on the ground underneath them and their breath hissed. The rain was cold on his skin and the forest was silent. It seemed all the world held its breath.

Another loud shrill horn blast echoed through the forest, closer still.

'Ride like your lives depend on it, you fools,' Roan shouted.

Kat rode to the edge of the hill. There was a long embankment that levelled on to an enormous field and on the other side of it stood the Bregfurjen Forest made up of tall trees that stretched toward the horizon.

A shrill wail of a horn sounded behind the trees in the distance sending birds into the air in all directions.

'What was that?' Katrina asked.

'The War Horns of the Barbarian hordes,' King Warrick said. 'Ready yourself my dear.'

Katrina tightened her grip on her reigns. She wore shiny golden armour with the king's crest across her breast plate. Her long golden curls fell past her shoulders over the red cape behind her. The king's guard tightened their formation around Katrina and the king.

'SOLDIER'S READY!' The king shouted. The knights of the kingdom lined up on the edge of the hill before the embankment in line with the king. Behind them the first and third cavalry lined up for miles, and behind them stood rows and rows of archers and infantry. The generals were dispersed amongst their troops as were the lords of the kingdom.

The Commander General shouted at the top of his voice from the other end of the army. The men cheered. He shouted something louder still and again the men cheered even louder.

'How did the barbarians know we were here?' Katrina asked. 'We only just arrived.'

'Scouts I am sure,' King Warrick replied. He glanced over at her with a raised eyebrow. 'You need not fear. Stay close to me.'

She nodded. She gave him a smile. Most people were reassured by her when she did that, but there was a wisdom behind the king's eyes that saw through her. She took in the size of their army. Her stomach did somersaults. She started nervously. The monotonous drumming of the barbarian horde reverberated through the ground, and all through her body.

The war horn blasted closer this time. The trees swayed from one end of the forest all the way to the other. The barbarians were coming.

'Who is that?' Katrina shouted.

Three riders broke through the edge of the forest.

'Envoys most likely,' the king said. 'One of them is a Barbarian.'

He drew his scope and peered through it.

'Travers?' he whispered.

'I beg your pardon your majesty?' Katrina said.

'It can't be,' the king muttered. 'And Calren!'

He looked up from the scope and then with wide eyes at Katrina, 'One of the riders is Calren.'

'May I see?' she asked. He handed her the scope. He appeared as though he had seen a ghost.

Katrina peeked through the scope. An old man she did not recognise. Calren, her beloved, and... 'TALON!'

'Who?' the king asked.

'Talon Telmache,' Katrina shouted. 'What on earth is he doing here?'

'Who is he?'

'A boy from my village. No, my – my best friend. He was guest of honour at our wedding!'

'What the goat is going on?'

'Why are they stopping?' Katrina shouted. 'They're stopping.'

The ground shook under the sound of thousands of hooves beating at full speed. Katrina's heart was in her throat. *Come on you fools. Come back to me.*

Talon pulled his horse to a stop. Roan and Calren did the same.

'What are you doing?' Roan shouted.

'That's Katrina up there,' he said. 'She's alive!'

'Alive?' Calren said.

'Let's go say hello then, shall we,'

Talon turned back towards the forest and stared at the tree tops rustling.

'The barbarians are almost here,' Roan said. 'We are almost home.'

'No more running,' Talon said.

'What are you talking about?' Calren said. 'My father's army will handle the rest.'

'No more being a coward,' Talon said.

'You don't need to avenge your woman anymore,' Roan said. 'She is waiting on that hill.'

'She is waiting for him,' Talon said nodding at Calren.

'There is no one to avenge boy!' Roan shouted.

'What about Amara?' Talon said. He twisted his face with rage. A deep anger boiled from within.

Roan dismounted Thayer and yanked Talon off of his horse.

'Prince Calren, please ride to your father, we will be behind you shortly,' Roan said. Calren nodded.

'I will tell her of your bravery. I will tell her it was you who rescued me. Our kingdom, I, owe you a great debt Talon Telmache,' Calren said. He turned and he rode off.

'Calren is coming,' Katrina said.

'First Platoon!' the king shouted. 'Retrieve the prince.'

They shouted and descended the embankment at an angle that would allow them to flank the prince and ride behind him for protection.

'What about Talon?' Katrina asked.

'They are too far out,' the king said.

'Please your majesty,' she said. 'I need to speak to him. He thinks I'm upset with him. I know him.'

'I cannot let you go to him,' the king said.

'He's my best friend,' she shouted. 'Please.'

'No one wants you to do this,' Roan said. 'No one expects it.'

'Exactly,' Talon said.

'Ah,' Roan exclaimed. 'I am arguing with a fool.'

He made to mount Thayer again, but the horse would not let him. He trotted over to Talon and turned in a circle and then bowed.

'Thayer?' Talon said. 'Are you with me old boy?'

The horsed neighed proudly. Talon mounted Thayer and found to his left his father's sword on Thayer's side. He unsheathed it and held it up. Thayer reared kicking his front legs out, then he reared again.

The barbarian riders broke through the forest edge.

'What is he doing?' Katrina asked, still peering through the scope.

Talon was looking up at her. He bowed his head and then raised what looked like his father's sword. *Thayer?*

'He's riding his father's horse, Captain Telmache's horse,'

'Telmache?' The king said. He nodded. 'He is going to charge them!'

'What? He can't do that.'

'He is either the biggest fool or the bravest man, my dear,' the king said. Katrina was unaware that tears were streaming down her cheeks.

'TALON!' She shouted. He looked up. "YOU COME BACK HERE RIGHT NOW!'

She peered through the scope. He smiled at her. That same goofy smile she loved so much.

'Please,' she whispered to herself. 'I'm sorry.'

Thayer turned and sped towards the barbarian army. A lonely white steed and young rider against a tidal wave of black. They were a mile or two apart.

'ARCHERS,' the king shouted. "COVER FIRE!'

'COVER FIRE!'

The sound of thousands of arrows launching into the air resounded over their heads.

'CAVALRY, ATTACK!' the king shouted. The men erupted into roars as the wave of horses descended the embankments. 'RIDE! RIDE! RIDE TO YOUR BRETHENS AID! RIDE TO TELMACHE! RIDE!'

Talon glanced back, Roan was behind him riding the other black horse.

'Someone has to keep you out of trouble you fool!' he shouted.

Talon smiled and raised his father's sword above his head. The skies went black. He looked up and found thousands upon thousands of arrows falling to the ground through the torrent. The first wave hit, and the entire front line of the barbarian cavalry fell. The riders behind them jumped over their fallen brethren.

The only thing Talon heard was the drumming of thousands upon thousands of hooves and the shouts of every man and barbarian on the field.

The second wave of arrows hit and sent the next round of barbarian cavalry screaming to the ground.

The next wave broke through those.

Talon closed his eyes. For a second he was in the cotton field holding Katrina. Another wave of arrows. The drumming of hooves. The barbarian war horn.

He was at his first dance. Kat was whispering a secret into his ear. She smiled at him.

The barbarian cavalry broke ranks and headed around them to flank them. Through the fray he spotted Drag'a. Talon lift his sword before all the barbarians and all his countrymen, before Roan and before Katrina. He pulled his sword back and Thayer broke into the column of barbarians. He aimed and with all his might flung his sword.

The force from another horse threw him off Thayer and sent him crashing to the ground.

'And it was with that fateful blow, that Talon Telmache strung the fatal blow, killing Drag'a,'

The hall erupted into resounding applause. King Warrick, Prince Calren and Princess Katrina stood and so did all the delegates in attendance. The applause continued on for another minute before dying down slowly.

The hall fell silent. Roan, the sage dressed in a fine crimson and gold robe had tears in his eyes. He scanned the room. Blithe Telmache, a fierce woman, sat stoic, tears in hers. She was a strong woman, but like Roan he could see her heart too was broken. A brunette girl sat next to her tears in her eyes as well. And across the room, Katrina's tears streamed down her cheeks.

Roan smiled. Princess Katrina wore the emerald necklace his mother had left him.

"for you to one-day give to your soulmate".

'When I met Talon Telmache, he was introduced to me as a coward. When I was there at the end I knew this not to be true. If he was indeed Talon the Coward, then he was the bravest coward that I ever knew.'

There was dead silence in the hall.

'Or perhaps not a coward at all. None are more so deserving of their title. To Talon Telmache, The Bravest of Us All.'

THE END

Lightning Source UK Ltd.
Milton Keynes UK
UKHW040637180521
383923UK00001B/69